I0648423

Alejandro Morales

Collected Plays

NoPassport Press

For performance enquiries contact: New Dramatists Alumni, 424 West 44th Street, NY, NY 10036 USA, e-mail: newdramatists.org, or e-mail: alex@packawallop.org

Cover photo: from Packwallop Productions' production of *expat/inferno*. Courtesy of Packwallop Productions.

NoPassport Press
Dreaming the Americas Series

Series Editors: Jorge Huerta, Otis Ramsey-Zoe, Caridad Svich
Advisory Board: Daniel Banks, Maria M. Delgado, Amparo Garcia-Crow, Randy Gener, Elana Greenfield, Sarah Cameron Sunde, Tamara Underiner

Other titles in this series include:
Oliver Mayer: Collected Plays
Anne Garcia-Romero: Collected Plays
Lorca: Major Plays Volume I & II translated by Caridad Svich

NoPassport Press
Is a division of theatre alliance NoPassport devoted to diversity, difference, And freedom of expression in theatre and performance with an emphasis on an embrace of the hemispheric spirit.

First edition 2007.
NoPassport
PO Box 1786
South Gate CA 90280 USA
e-mail: NoPassportPress@aol.com

ISBN: 978-0-6151-8621-4
$19.95 paperback.

Acknowledgements

The three plays in this volume would not have been possible without the following people. They all made significant contributions to the material in workshops, conversations and production. In ways both grand and small they were stewards and champions of my work. I am forever in their debt.

Liz Duffy Adams, Maggie Boffil, Justin Bond, Sheila Callaghan, Christen Clifford, Drew Cortese, Jorge Ignacio Cortiñas, Jennie Crotero, Alma Cuervo, Tripp Cullman, Judith Delgado, John Dias, Annie Dorsen, Mark H. Dold, Peter du Bois, Greg Emetaz, Amy Feinberg, Michael-John Garcés, Anne Garcia Romero, Tarah Grant, Logan Marshall Green, Kelly Gregson, Kelly Grider, Jason Griffin, David Grimm, Zabryna Guevara, Mercedes Herrero, Elena K. Holy, Inez, Celise Kalke, Michael Kenyon, Mahayana Landowne, Ron Lasko, Nathan Lively, Alison Lowander, Florencia Lozano, Lulu, Lorenzo Mans, Honor Molloy, Maggie Moore, Ramon de Ocampo, Lisa Portes, Gary Prottas, Rick de Rochères, Rebecca Rugg, Debbie Saivetz, Seaweed, Betty Shamieh, Jeff Sundheim, Caridad Svich, Carmelita Tropicana, Eduardo Vega, Matthew Waldman, Jessica Watters. Nathan M. White, Jo Winiarski.

I want to especially thank Dean Harris for a great deal, but most particularly for introducing me to Antonioni, Fellini, Dario Argento, and Mario Bava. *marea* would not have been written without him being in my life.

My fellow writers and the staff of New Dramatists provided me with a home and endless source of support for seven years. I grew up as a writer in that building and these plays all benefited greatly by my tenure there. Thank you Todd London, Emily Morse, Paul Slee, Joel Ruark, Karen Noyes, Ron Riley, Jennie Greer, Melissa Kievman, John Steber and everyone else who has passed through that building in the last seven years.

My friends and colleagues at Packawallop Productions are my source of strength and inspiration. Marc Solomon, Susan Louise O'Connor, Polly Lee, Julian Stetkevych, Travis York, Barry Hitchcock, and Kari Bentley-Quinn have repeatedly proved their mettle as friends and fellow creatives. I cannot imagine my life without them.

My best friend and constant collaborator Scott Ebersold must be singled out. He has read scraps, has commented on stray monologues, and pored over terrible first drafts repeatedly. He has been my champion when I have needed it the most. He makes me a better writer and a better artist.

Finally, I'd like to thank my family. My aunt Ana Baez and my grandfather Juan Antonio Morales continue to cheer me on and have generously contributed to Packawallop. My mother Magali Barral and my father Juan Francisco Morales encouraged my love of writing and theater from an early age and have often flown to New York even just to see a reading. My father has also read everything I've written and has often been an invaluable source of information, encouragement and feedback. Thank you to my brother Juan Carlos Morales for just being the coolest.

Lastly, I'd like to thank my grandmother Elia Velazquez. The amount of support she gave me was immeasurable. I miss her greatly.

Contents

'Haunted Islands'

Alejandro Morales

In conversation with Caridad Svich

[Cuban-American playwright Alejandro Morales revels in the kind of *mestizaje* laid down by his playwriting forebears (Latino and otherwise). Morales exhibits in his writing a free-flowing, heavily cinematic structure similar to dramatist Naomi Iizuka's, and an obsessive, darkly humorous mix of high and low tonalities similar to Jose Rivera's. His work also is deeply indebted to film master Pedro Almodovar, whose explosive and rarefied vision has indelibly marked the Latino sensibility. Morales in his plays *sebastián, marea and expat/inferno* is writing primarily about identity and specifically a trifurcated queer Cuban identity that is Spanish, French and US. Although the specter of Federico Garcia Lorca also appears in Morales' work as both poetic marker and actualised presence, what distinguishes his writing is his complex grappling with notions of exile and the role of the expatriate within an exile community. In his play *expat/inferno* produced in New York's fringe festival in 2003, Dante's *Inferno* becomes the template for a meditation on life in New York City post 9/11/01, where dreams of an imagined torch-song-filled Paris may or may not provide refuge.

In Morales' work the internal and external geographies of migration are always in flux. His characters cannot rest because they belong neither here nor there but rather in-between, in the limbic space of dreams and transition. For Morales, personal and political upheaval for the Latino is the rule rather than the exception, and success, if found, is marginal at best. Morales' worldview speaks to his condition as an exiled American, and moreover as an exiled emerging avant-garde artist. This interview was initially conducted via e-mail late 2003, and revised for publication in the fall of 2007. – Caridad Svich]

CS: Your plays are populated with spectral figures and environments. Saints and ghosts inhabit your plays and your characters' dreams. Loss is often at the heart of this spectral preoccupation: loss of a beloved, a country, a language... What draws you to theatrically portraying absence in presence? And how do these writing journeys, in plays like *sebastián*, and *expat/inferno*, begin for you?

AM: One of my earliest memories was attending a meeting of *espiritistas* at my great-grandmother's house. My great-grandmother was the oldest person I knew and was infinitely mysterious to me, sitting in that darkened living room, calling forth the dead. Although I couldn't understand what was happening when were told a "presence" was among us, I felt change in the darkness. The air vibrated, messages were delivered, and my imagination was sparked. Looking back, that the room was probably filled with a great many ghosts because Cubans are a haunted people. They live with a great deal of nostalgia. I'm sure many of them were trying to recapture something they desired and lost—a home, another life, a family member they've been separated from. Were the presences I felt actual spirits or just the intensity of the longing shared by everyone present?

Theatrically speaking, I've always been interested in recreating my great grandmother's living room. I love when invisible elements manifest on stage among the solid and living. These invisible elements are rooted in a character's internal life, which the audience becomes privy to through the reading of postcards, internal monologues, or third-person narration of a thought process. But like the people who sought out my grandmother's spiritual help, sometimes my characters' desires become so great they manifest in dream or phantom figures.

For example, *expat/inferno* was inspired by the process of getting through a breakup while New York City was engaged in a post 9/11 grief. There was a part of me that wanted to deny the experience, to make things as they once were. So I wrote a story about this guy who is denial that 9/11 happened or that it has affected him personally. Danny tries to forget the present by running to the past, so the memories he conjures up—his lover X, his mother, a trip to Paris, the face of a woman on a missing person's flier—take over the play. I've always felt each character in *expat/inferno* is a manifestation of Danny's psyche. His trip to Paris, like Dante's trip to the Inferno, is an allegorical one.

Like *expat/inferno, marea* employs a spectral figure in order for the protagonist to question how she remembers a personal history obscured by elements in her day to day life. Maria, a Cuba-born woman living in New York, denies her past by immersing herself in 1960s Italian cinema. She dates a woman named after a character in an Antonioni film and drinks chianti, smokes cigarettes and listens to Nino Rota. However, she is confronted with the ghost of her mother, who appears in the guise of a 1960s Italian gothic horror film actress. Maria has confused her memories with movies and her history appears disguised as fiction to make her reevaluate herself. I took the work I did in *marea* farther when I adapted one of those 1960s Italian horror films, *castle of blood*. Practically everyone except the main character is dead—his self-destructive nature is underscored by the dead people who surround him try to kill him so they can drink his blood.

sebastián was another matter entirely, because the main character is a flesh and blood person who has to deal with the other characters projecting their desires onto him. Each time this happens, he usually starts to bleed. He is cut open more and more until he becomes so porous he disappears at the end of the play. Similarly, in my first play, in *the silent concerto*, the three characters project their desires onto themselves by performing in improvised playlets performed for each other or an imaginary audience. The ending of that play involves a reverse theatrical transformation as all three characters step out of the play they've been living in for the past two hours and enter the very real, very ugly, very physical theater the play was being performed in. They realize their imaginary audience is not there. They stop being "characters" and become real people, flawed and awkward, as they bow to the emptiness.

CS: *sebastián* is set in Havana, *expat/inferno* is set in Paris and New York, and *sweaty palms* in Granada. Although the locations are geographically different, there is in your depiction of these places a similar sense of emptiness, of cities bordered by chaos and upheaval yet existing in a feverish and isolated manner in relationship to their citizens. How do you feel land marks a body (a single body, and the body politic of a given country) and therefore affects cultural memory?

AM: Growing up I believed Cuba was the most terrifying place on earth. My family told me all about the buildings in ruin, ration booklets, forced labor in sugar cane fields, and a demonic figure named Fidel Castro. I grew up with a dark image of a country I imagined in detail, yet never visited. In marea, Maria imagines Cuba as a vampire film. In *sebastián*, Cuba is depicted as an island of whores and orphans. My theatrical descriptions of Cuba are reminiscent of Proust's descriptions of Venice in the first volume of *A Remembrance of Things Past*. Proust suggests is that imagining a place can often be as insightful as actually visiting it. My imagined Cuba became an entity as real and as potent as the island 90 miles away from South Florida. This imagined Cuba is the setting of *sebastián* and the place where Maria and her grandmother Regla come from.

The interesting thing Normally, I don't have a pressing interest in making sociopolitical commentary when I start writing a play, but it is inevitable that such commentary emerges if I pay close attention to my characters and how their environment affects them. For example, *sweaty palms* began as a desire to explore the poetic and surrealistic aspects of Garcia Lorca's life and work. I became intrigued by a figure from "Poema del cante jondo (Poem of the Deep Song)" named Amargo, a dark force who can see into the very marrow of anyone he encounters. This Lorquian figure inspired his namesake in *sweaty palms* – a Gypsy who torments his half-sister Leonora. As I wrote the play and explored Amargo and Leonora's relationship, I realized these characters embodied the struggle between the anarchic/socialist Left and the conservative Right in 1930s Spain. Amargo dreams of claiming his birthright—the olive groves belonging to his late father, while Leonora attempts to maintain a sense of the propriety as war and a blossoming sexuality invade her life. The play became less and less about Lorca's poetic figures and more about how the repression of personal freedoms ends up destroying a society (also a Lorquian theme). All the characters in *sweaty palms* end up broken by the end of the play, much in the same way Spain was by Franco's victory in the war. When I wrote the first draft of the play, I had not visited the play's setting, Granada. In between drafts, I visited Spain and was amazed by how much Spain resembled the version I had created in *sweaty palms*.

The sociopolitical content of *expat/inferno* emerged somewhat differently. I originally began with a desire to write about heartbreak in Paris, a city typically associated with romance. The play was populated with Americans in Paris, fleeing the US for various personal reasons. As I was writing a scene that took place on an airplane, September 11 happened. I realized it was impossible to proceed without acknowledging this event. There was much talk about patriotism in the news and what it meant to be an American. A play about Americans in a foreign place resonated differently as all Americans found themselves in a metaphysically foreign place—America was no longer the same after that Tuesday. I subsequently read an essay by Saul Bellow about the Lost Generation, which opened up a new way of thinking about Americans in Paris. He said, "In Paris, they were free to be truly American." And I began to see the play as an example of how being in a foreign place can allow one to truly achieve a stronger sense of identity. The two Beatrices find their respective nationalities growing more extreme when they are away from home and Danny comes to accept truths about himself and his lover X by escaping his home and journeying to Paris.

As the son of immigrants, I find Bellow's statement intriguing. I find that the relationship to geography seems to echo a great deal among many other Latino writers as political upheaval and emigration are cornerstones of our experience. Our identities are constantly examined because we exist as "the other" in the US. I wonder if my family became more Cuban in the United States, when it became imperative for them to remember their customs and language in the push to adapt to a new setting and way of life. *marea* is concerned with this issue. How much of where we come from and what we inherit from ur parents affects how our lives end up—even when one may try to deny and run away from all that is one's history or culture.

The play posits that such denial is impossible. Who we are, where we come from and where we live are intimately linked.

My newest play, *the october crisis (to laura)*, developed in an interesting way. When my grandmother died, I thought a great deal about the relationships between mothers and sons—something not foreign to my work. When I thought about the fact that my father left his mother to come to the United States in 1962, shortly before the Missile Crisis, it became clear to me I had to set the play in 1962 and deal with Cuba in some way because Cuba and the year 1962 were part of my father's story as it relates to his mother. None of the characters in the play are Cuban, but the combination of a pre-Castro Havana and a Kennedy era U.S. were my way into this story about a dying woman and her estranged son.

CS: Intense quick sexual encounters punctuate or drive forward many of your plays. Characters communicate one thing through sex and yet another when they speak. And the action of the discrete scenes in your work often hinges upon the betrayals that occur intentionally and unintentionally between actions read by body and those read by the mind. What do you think is your role as a writer in depicting sexuality on stage? And have you ever been misinterpreted in your aims in this regard by audiences or critics?

AM: When I was in college, I studied 17th Century sculptor Pietro Bernini's

The Ecstasy of Saint Theresa of Avila. The sculpture employs theatrical

scenic and lighting elements to depict St. Theresa being penetrated by an

angel's "dart of divine love." Her ecstasy is spiritual, but Bernini is clearly

influenced by the sensual descriptions of holy visions in Theresa's writing.

Bernini's Theresa is a woman in the throes of sexual pleasure. That the

"ecstasy" of the title can be read as spiritual or sexual was striking to me.

Ecstasy can pulverize logic and self-control–an equally attractive and

repulsive concept to my bookish, Type A self.

   "I do what is appropriate," Leonora says to Amargo minutes before

she succumbs to his sexual advances in *sweaty palms*. This sense of what is

appropriate vs. what one desires is obviously a familiar concept to gay men

and lesbians. Because of this, I am especially sensitive to how desire relates

to–and often overrides–proper conduct. In the United States, we are

bombarded with sexual imagery in our advertising and pop culture, yet the

idea of sexual autonomy, especially for gays, is still a foreign concept.

Sexuality is merely a means to sell CDs or deodorant. A sophisticated

discussion about non-airbrushed sex makes the censors descend like

vultures … even if that discussion is clearly intended for adults. As far as

gay-themed plays go, I have found so many of them fit into this particular trend—they are either sentimental iterations of sitcom humor or they feature a gimmicky full frontal scene. There is much parading and little ecstasy.

So I return to Theresa. I am more and more fascinated by the danger of her transcendence. Sexual encounters can be dangerous because they contain the seed of emotional exposure. This is the kind of naked I prefer to see in the theater. In *expat/inferno*, Danny cannot talk about what happened to X without revealing his grief. He denies his heartbreak repeatedly until he picks up a stranger in Café Amnesia in Paris. Danny so desperately wants to recreate the experience of being in Paris with X, he stays in the very same hotel room he and X shared. The sequence in the play finds Danny waking up from a series of nightmares, as X and Kenny (his trick from Café Amnesia) alternate being next to him. During this exchange, Kenny and Danny discuss the sex they just had. I chose to graphically describe the sexual act to highlight that the physical encounter leaves Danny with no choice but to open up. He tells Kenny about some of his longing for X. It isn't much, but it's the most the audience has heard up to that point. Kenny and Danny end up repeating the words "I love you" to each other hoping that "if you say it enough you believe it." Danny breaks down in Kenny's arms at the thought of those "I love you's" he wishes he could say to X. The entire sequence has always made me somewhat uncomfortable because so little is obscured. But Danny experiences a moment of ecstacy in the way Bernini envisioned it.

The fact that gay characters and sexuality populate my plays makes them a hard sell to theaters. I get requests from theaters to send in *sebastián* all the time, but the play often gets sent back with deep regrets that the sexual nature of the play would not be appropriate subject matter for their subscribers. It's an issue I won't bend on. Investigating sexuality is a huge obsession of mine and obsessions contain the best material. Nonetheless, while I used to feel like I could thumb my nose at such conservative attitudes, I think the rightward migration of American popular culture has pretty much halted my career. It amazed me that during the last production of *the silent concerto* (2007) some straight couples marched out of the theater after Naldo and Benny innocently kiss. My co-producers and I tried to figure out a way to attract a gay audience, but that seemed impossible for some reason (coincidentally the *New York Times* ran an article on the growing difficulty of attracting gay audiences to theater while we were working on the show). I've responded by going subversively retro. My last two plays have featured my revisions of two loathsome stereotypes from gay plays past—*castle of blood*'s homicidal lesbian and *the october crisis (to*

laura)'s alcoholic, self-destructive closet case. Neither is able to be fully
expressed and from an artistic standpoint, I empathize.

CS: Like you, I am a hyphenated American writer. I grew up bilingually and
Spanish and English have always been a part of my life. When I began to
write for the theatre, I suddenly realized that to some extent I had to make a
conscious choice about which language I wanted to speak in as a writer,
which in turn would somehow dictate the audience I thought I was writing
for? Of course the more we write the more we realize that we speak many
languages at once on the page. How do you negotiate bi-ligualism and bi-
culturalism when you work, if at all?

AM: The issue of language was always crucial and I suspect my experience
is similar to that of many first-generation Latinos. While it was very
important to my family that I spoke English well, it was equally important
that I spoke Spanish with equal fluency. Both languages meant different
things—English equaled opportunity, while Spanish equaled identity. I
think this has given me an appreciation for the importance of expression and
communication. Being bilingual allowed me a sensitivity to translation and
the subtle (or overt) changes it brings about. So while I choose to write in
English, I find myself incorporating other languages into the fabric of my
plays. *sweaty palms* and *sebastián* take place in Spain and Cuba,

respectively. In those plays, I found certain Spanish words and phrases were untranslatable into English (i.e., Connie talking about "jineteras" or Leonora threatening to call "la guardia civil") so I didn't translate them. In the opening of sweaty palms, the Gypsy Venenosa sings a song whose lyrics I pieced together from Gypsy sayings found during research ("todos los trabajos son para las pobres mujeres"). It was my intention that the song evoke the lament of the "cante jondo" Lorca wrote about. I wanted it to invoke the emotional turmoil that vibrates in a flamenco singer. A translation would change the way the language resonates in the actress' body and strip the words of their authenticity. A translation would allow an English speaking audience to *understand* Venenosa, but they would not *feel* on a gut level. In fact, I tried it both ways in two different workshops, and my instincts were confirmed.

I expanded this idea in *marea* and *expat/inferno*. Both plays address the concept of translation. *expat/inferno* is about Danny, a Latino who has "forgotten" all his Spanish and must learn French to negotiate his way around Paris. Jacques Brel's "Ne Me Quitte Pas" figures throughout the play as does Rod McKuen's translation, "If You Go Away." Like Venenosa's lament, the song changes when translated and there was something about that change that spoke to Danny's dilemma. He needed to discover things about himself—his "true memories" not the poor translations he made of them. In *marea*, Maria is a Latina with a fascination for Italian art films of the 60s, most of which are dubbed or subtitled. Since Maria confuses her memories with movies, I wanted to explore how to depict those memories in a way appropriate to her character. The idea struck me to use Spanish in those scenes and explore ways to subtitle the dialogue delivery. In both workshops of the play, we used a female voice working like a UN translator, which added to the surrealism of the play.

CS: Garcia Lorca is an influential theatrical figure for both of us. He appears in your work, explicitly and in disguise. I know that every time I translate his work I learn so much about structure, time and space in theatre. This is true anytime you are in dialogue with a master artist. What have you learned from Lorca, and what are you building upon when consciously working within a Lorquian tradition, as in your play *sweaty palms*, for instance, and *sebastián*?

AM: When I was 17, I saw a production of *Blood Wedding*. Having never heard of Lorca before, the production was a total surprise and revelation. I was amazed at Lorca's theatrical world where dreams and desires invade reality. When the Moon appeared seeking blood, I could not believe how terrifying and sensual the language was. In university, I performed the scene in Spanish. I felt the words resonate in my ankles, my belly, the top of my skull. As an actor, only Shakespeare has done that to me. I realized the power of theatrical language studying Lorca and I feel eternally indebted to him for inspiring me to take up a pen and attempt the creation of such language myself.

When I set out to write my first play, *sweaty palms*, I wanted to connect with the most authentic aspects of myself. The first thing I did was promise to sign the play "Alejandro Morales" and not my more casual moniker, "Alex." The second was to incorporate Lorca into the play because my desire to be a playwright stemmed from him. I had just een "The Disappearance of Garcia Lorca," a film which I did not like very much and I felt I had to avenge Federico somehow (I was 23 and subject to that sort of thing). I began thinking about his death and the historical events surrounding it. So, I knew the play had to be set in Granada, 1936. In researching Lorca's writings on his childhood in Granada, I discovered Amargo, a character from Lorca's "Poema del cante jondo," who became the inspiration for my Amargo. While Lorca's Amargo was an enigmatic specter, my version was all too aware of his lot in life. He is the product of an illicit love affair between a rich landowner and his Gypsy servant. His dream of inheriting his father's olive groves diminishes as the Spanish Civil

War rages and his skin blossoms with bruises. By the play's end, he recites lines from Lorca's "Fabula y rueda de los tres amigos," a poem that eerily predicted Lorca's demise. Even though Lorca does not figure as a character in this play, it was impossible to write about Granada and not feel his presence. Visiting Granada for research, I found him everywhere—the Alhambra, the Albaicín, and most definitely in Fuente Vaqueros where his childhood home stands. As Leonora rushes to escape Spain, Amargo is left behind, certain to crumble and vanish in the Franco regime that extinguished both Lorca and the revolutionary personal freedoms he envisioned in his plays and poetry.

While writing *sebastián*, I was interested in this character named Federico. An amnesiac running through contemporary Havana in a white suit, he seemed too similar to the real Lorca for my taste. Why was Lorca in a play set in contemporary Havana? If this is Lorca, what does he do to the fabric of the play? I didn't want the play to be a metaphysical story about Lorca's ghost. However, the character would not leave my imagination. I accepted my obsession and temporarily let go of my concerns. I kept working on the play and eventually discovered my Federico was not the author of *Yerma* or *Romancero gitano*. He was an entirely fictional character who borrowed the identity of Lorca and an anecdote from his biography—Lorca's visit to Havana. When Lorca visited Havana, no one knows exactly what he got up to, but apparently the visit changed him profoundly. Many suspect his sexual adventures with the mulattos on the island where a panacea to his lingering depression and he returned to Spain ready to write his great works. I became intrigued by this conception of Havana as miracle. A place where having your wishes granted would fix whatever was broken inside you. The title character and protagonist of the play solidified thanks to Federico's yearning for him. Sebastián becomes like one of the white screens in the bordello where he works, where people project their desires and fantasies. He begins to bleed when touched and eventually vanishes as others' projections eclipse what is left of him. Sebastián is a continuation of Amargo. His disappearance suggests the decay and crumbling of Havana as result of warring ideologies.

While Lorca has been a profound influence on me, I also value the time I've spent exploring other artists such as Marcel Proust, Stephen Sondheim, Tori Amos, Michelangelo Antonioni or Pedro Almodóvar. Like you said, there is value in learning from a master artist. *Blood Wedding,* "L'Avventura" and "The Law of Desire" have been some of my greatest teachers. By engaging with these artists in my plays, I am able to discover greater personal truths because I am figuring out what it is in me that responds to these works. I also feel that it is essential to understand what precedes you artistically. We don't create in a vacuum. These artists have gone before and charted territory so that we may travel through it and discover what lies beyond.

CS: Your work is also populated with characters obsessed by or working inside pop forms, such as cabaret and drag. There is often a delicate ironic commentary you make as writer between the concrete Pop world and the less concrete, less manage-able sometimes "real" world that your fictions create. What attracts you to examining the performative act within a play?

AM: As a writer I am drawn to the way people perform their various selves. I suppose it's an easy deduction to make that gay people have an inherent understanding of life as performance. Out of necessity, we all perform different versions of ourselves depending on the level of acceptance we're surrounded with, including an attempt to "perform" as straight for some portion of our lives. When I became sexually active in college, I was so divorced from my sexual self I often felt I had to assume a completely different persona whenever I had sex. Sebastián, Amargo, and all the split women who populate my work are a result of that.

In recognizing the way I perform in my day-to-day life, I have a deep empathy for performers in general. I'm particularly drawn to the archetypical suffering divas such as Maria Callas, La Lupe, Dusty

Springfield, Edith Piaf, Judy Garland, and Tori Amos. Part of this is my

opera loving father's doing, but I think my fascination stems from something

else. These women suffered heartbreak, rape, miscarriages, and addiction

but they'd stand in front of an audience and turn the ugly things they've

suffered into beauty. There is alchemy at work in the image of a tragic

singer. To date, I have written three plays with singers in them—*sebastián,*

expat/inferno and *the october crisis (to laura)*. All three of these women

wrestle with that alchemy and they are each broken down even to the point

of death. I suppose there is a part of me that endows these women with the

parts of being an artist that frighten me. I worry about the amount of

sacrifices I have to make in order to write. I worry about what it'll cost me

eventually to pursue a life where I can be creative. The fear is so great that

it spurs me on to unearth all the fabulousness I am capable of.

There is no play in my body of work that encapsulates that fear more

than *the silent concerto*. All three characters have very real, very scary

insecurities to deal with, particularly their fear of failure. All three of them

are theatrical, so they deal with their insecurities by adopting these grand

personas and engaging with each other mostly through a series of theatrical

turns. The greater their fear of the real world becomes, the more theatrical their behavior and unreal the world they inhabit. My favorite moment comes in the first movement of the play. In an effort to employ various theatrical tropes to further the characters' relationships, I felt there needed to be a production number ala "Good Morning Good Morning" from "Singing in the Rain." Since the first movement takes place in the early 90s, I had Mallory kickstart the production number by lipsync-ing to Tori Amos's "Crucify." The moment is hysterically funny and then joyous as all three characters join in the dance. There is then a poignancy as their abandon is coupled with Amos's lyrics about being constantly broken down in her attempts to find love and integrity in her life. All three create a mini MGM musical out of fears none of them could admit to each other. They are temporarily transported until the tape player eats the tape, rudely hurtling them back into an uncommunicative reality.

CS: Throughout history theatre practitioners have been called upon to be the ones with the vantage point to critique, comment on, or affect change in society. It seems as if in this country at least the role of the theatre artist has become more and more, except for very few, rare cases, one where all that is expected is for the artist to entertain the public, or tell a good story. Now, both of these are commendable tasks and a necessary part of our job as writers, but do you feel is it our only job? In other words, do you see yourself as having a responsibility as an artist which goes beyond the telling of a story, and if so, what is that role and how do you envision it?

AM: When Ingmar Bergman and Michelangelo Antonioni died recently (2007), I remember being shocked at some of the sentiments expressed in some of the tributes written in their honor. Some people went so far as to imply that these two men would have been nothing had their not been a cult built around the European avant-garde in the late 1950s/early 60s. I was angered by what I initially interpreted as a denial of the great talent these two men had, but then realized what some of these writers were really saying is that our contemporary cultural climate would not allow an Antonioni or a Bergman to achieve the superstar prominence they had when they made their great films.

My life has been changed the most by the works of art that have truly challenged me at various points in my life—Antonioni's "L'Avventura," Proust's *In Search of Lost Time*, David Lynch's "Mulholland Drive" are all great examples. They all showed me there was a way to look at the world differently by challenging my expectations as a spectator. Works of art that challenge expectations don't seem to be encouraged a whole lot these days. I recently read a quote by Roundabout Theater artistic director Todd Haimes where he discusses the recent trend of adapting films into plays. He said "there has been a swing backward in the past decade toward audiences enjoying traditional stories as opposed to avant-garde things that were more popular in the '70s" as a justification as to why this sort of theatrical recycling is taking place. I probably took that quote a lot more personally than I should have, but as I look at the current theatrical climate I see little room for my work in it *because* of this "swing backward."

In the context of the article, Haimes's quote seems to imply he just wants to "give the people what they want." But this is the way commercial theater operates. Not-for-profit theaters have missions that must do more than just meet the demands of the marketplace (which is *why* they are not-for profit in the first place). It's unfortunate the concept behind not-for-profit theater is virtually non-existent. I run a small not-for-profit company with my best friend Scott Ebersold. It's a struggle for us to get funding to do *one* production a year, but that *one* production is something we feel challenges us both the artists and the audience. A potential board member asked us why we didn't abandon the non-profit model and start a commercial venture. I pointed out that a commercial producer would take one look at my work, see a gay character and pass. I couldn't become that kind of producer. I couldn't let our company operate solely based on "what sells." I believe in our *obligation* to be of service not only to our audience but to the artists who are creating work and therefore ensuring the development of the medium.

I wouldn't have any interest in writing if all I was expected to do were to entertain or tell a good story. Being a playwright is such a challenging career. In fact, I would go so far as to say it is a vocation (like being a monk with an office job). With little promise of economic reward, I write plays because they are *necessary*. I always have to ask myself why each play I write needs to be written. If I am going to devote hours of my free time working on something, it better be incredibly important. And if it's not important to me initially how can I expect anyone to find my work important enough to fork over an admissions fee and two hours of their lives?

I am troubled by the lack of importance and funding the arts are given in this country. I am troubled by the conservative cultural shift the country has undergone since the first Bush administration. I am troubled by how homogenous the audience for theater is becoming and therefore ensuring that only voices that appeal to upper middle class urban whites are heard. I am troubled that people don't read unless Oprah tells them too. My work can't possibly address all these things, but many of the choices I make both as a writer and as a producer are dictated by my responses to these trends.

Perhaps it's quixotic, idealistic and foolish to do so, but I don't think I know of any other way to be an artist.

CS: Risking failure every day is what we do as practitioners. It is in many ways critical to our work to be able to risk failure and understand fully what that risk is as we face the page or walk into a practice hall. What strategies do you have for embracing failure (and I use the word, obviously, in a positive sense)?

AM: The last production of *the silent concerto* was incredibly challenging for me as a writer and a producer. Both Scott and I worked very long and hard on this play while working full time day jobs. We were met with casting challenges, terrible weather, poor box office, audience walkouts, a no-show from the *New York Times* and a handful of early reviews that crippled me artistically for months. After the show closed, I was unable to write for a good many months. This is unusual for me as I'm a very consistent and steady writer. However, I felt I couldn't trust myself. If there were people who despised *the silent concerto*, a play I felt such a strong personal commitment to, what does that say about other plays with which I connected?

I'm incredibly ambitious and incredibly hard on myself. I worry about every rejection letter and worry about how my work is perceived (i.e., "he can't get a *real* theater to produce him, he has to self-produce!"). I worry if my work isn't honest enough or if it's banal or conventional. I worry about what to say when someone asks me "have I heard of anything you've written?" I worry about people in my family telling my parents, "I told you so! He should have gone to law school!" But none of these worries compared to the months following *the silent concerto* where I just couldn't write at all.

I had to enter into a small agreement with myself. I promised I would write for 20 minutes every day and just let myself write "crap." I'd rather write crap every day than not write at all. As of this writing, I am 65 pages into *the october crisis (to laura)* which was the result of all that crappiness. These 65 pages will be read as part of my graduation at New Dramatists in a few weeks (October 2007). I started getting nervous when I gave the play to Scott for the first time. What if it actually *is* crap? What will I do then? Ironically, I thought of *the silent concerto*. My job wasn't to receive applause. My job was to show up, serve drinks, tear tickets, give a curtain speech, move the set (all in a day's work for the co-Artistic Director of a small company). When I think about the specifics of my work as a playwright, it may not make the fear of failure go away, but it focuses me enough to actually *do* the work.

Mothers are often at the center of my work. My mother is quite a massive force in my life. Her commitment to my brother and me is astounding and that commitment is enough to have her keep on being our mother even when things get rocky. She got us dressed and fed and drove us to school. She took care of us when we were sick and took it in stride when we had our little tantrums. I like to follow her example when it comes to my work. I think being maternal with the plays allows me to connect with what I love about them and forgive them when they fall short of my expectations. Like children, plays need time to learn how to speak and walk and grow up. Sometimes they'll stumble, but it's my job to pick them up again and get them back on track.

sebastián
a play by alejandro morales

developed at new dramatists, intar new works lab, the public theater new work now. winner whitfield cook award 2003

characters:

sebastián: a dark skinned youth no older than 21. he is extremely beautiful, but tense, like a coiled spring. he could equally be capable of extreme tenderness or violence, which is part of his charm.

federico: a spaniard in his forties. haunted and lost, yet not entirely noble. his skin pale, almost sick. his eyes, completely black and indiscernible.

connie: a woman in her forties who only wishes she's seen better days. her body is not her greatest charm. instead, her imagination runs rampant, making her seem like a ghost wandering a time that is not her own.

benito: a young man no older than 21. his skin is fair, rather delicate. he is secretive and one's first impression is likely to be mistaken.

saints and martyrs:

saint sebastian: roman christian martyr. sebastian was a captain of the praetorian guard but was also secretly a christian who made many converts. when the roman emperor diocletian learned of his faith, he ordered sebastian shot to death by archers. the arrows did not kill him, however, and a christian widow named irene took him away and tended his wounds. as soon as he recovered, sebastian returned to the emperor and denounced him for his cruelty. diocletian then ordered him beaten to death (and probably raped, depending on who you read). the first martyrdom of saint sebastian was a favorite subject for italian painters of the renaissance usually because it allowed for depiction of male nudity, therefore, saint sebastián and his lore have acquired a homoerotic resonance.

saint agnes: according to a 6th-century legend, agnes was a beautiful roman girl who refused marriage because of her dedication to christ. after rejecting many suitors, she was denounced as a christian and sent to a house of prostitution as her punishment. when a young man ventured to touch her, he lost his sight, but he then regained it in answer to her prayers. shortly thereafter she was executed and buried on the via nomentana in a catacomb eventually named for her.

la caridad del cobre (our lady of charity): a statue of the virgin mary found off the coast of cobre, a cuban mining town. she is revered throughout the island as a miracle worker and many flock to her shrine to offer gifts in exchange for miracles. she is also the catholic stand-in for oshún, the goddess of love, in santería.

federico garcía lorca: spanish poet and playwright executed by the falangist forces during the spanish civil war in 1936. he visited cuba after a long period of depression in the 1920s and emerged a changed man, going on to write his greatest works upon his return to spain. he was deeply enamored of the country, especially because of the (largely undocumented) sexual exploits he was able to have there with the countless young *mulato* men he encountered.

setting:

the play takes place in contemporary havana, usually in la iglesia, a run down church that serves as a private cabaret for tourists. by law, these seat no more than 12.

1.

(federico, a man in his forties, wearing an immaculately-pressed white suit and neatly slicked-back hair is on the street. havana is experiencing a blackout. sebastián, a young man appears. he's dressed casually, but everything about his appearance suggests a beautiful brutality.)

sebastián: hey.

federico: no, thank you.

sebastián: what the hell is that supposed to mean?

federico: they warned me at the hotel.

sebastián: warned you?

federico: people will try to sell you things.

sebastián: did i say i was selling something? i just want to talk.

federico: nobody just wants to talk.

sebastián: what if i say i followed you from your hotel?

federico: i'd be worried.

sebastián: you scared?

federico: it's too dark.

sebastián: don't the streets get dark like this in spain?

federico: is that where i'm from?

sebastián: i don't know. are you?

federico: of course ... what i meant is ... how'd you know?

sebastián: the way you talk.

federico: i don't think it gets this dark in spain … or anywhere else. how can anyone see?

sebastián: you learn. there's probably several people looking at us right now.

federico: *(looking around.)* where?

sebastián: doesn't matter. i ain't doing nothing wrong. just talking to a tourist about the wonders of this island.

federico: and the darkness …

sebastián: we're saving electricity. besides, we can have much more fun this way.

(shoves federico to the ground.)

federico: this is very unfair. i can't see you.

sebastián: i'm not the one wearing the white suit.

federico: you don't like it?

sebastián: i hate it.

federico: you've got something against suits?

sebastián: just the white ones.   i thought you were a ghost.

federico: did i scare you?

sebastián: i've seen ghosts before.

federico: i suppose it's fair to admit that you almost scare me, too.

sebastián: *(laughing.)* almost?

federico: look, i'll give you anything you want if you just leave me alone.

sebastián: anything i want? how about you answer some questions?

federico: what kind of questions?

sebastián: where're you going?

federico: just taking a walk.

sebastián: where?

federico: no place.

sebastián: i don't believe you.

federico: i wanted to see the *malecón*.

sebastián: that's over by the water and that ain't anywhere near here. just say it. you're lost.

federico: no.

(sebastián presses federico up against a wall.)

federico: you're crushing me.

sebastián: say it.

federico: alright, i'm lost. i've forgotten the way back to my hotel.

sebastián: *(letting him go.)* good.

federico: i forget things from time to time. i can't remember how i got here. it was like i woke up, looking at the customs officer. he asked me my occupation. i said, "business man."

sebastián: what kind of business?

federico: who knows? inventor, i guess. i remember the name on the officer's tag. minoz. i don't know if that means something. he just looked at my passport and gave it back to me, letting me into the island. to do what, i don't know.

sebastián: *(laughing and turning to leave.)* well, maybe you can figure it out.

federico: where are you going?

sebastián: nowhere you need to know about.

federico: at least show me back to my hotel. this is the most terrifying place i've ever been.

sebastián: i don't want to show you back anywhere.

federico: i'd pay you.

sebastián: i don't need your money.

federico: i can tell you're hungry.

sebastián: what's it to you?

federico: why'd you stop me?

sebastián: i was bored.

federico: and this is what you do for fun?

sebastián: only with white suits.

federico: what's this suit done to you?

sebastián: a lot.

(federico turns on his lighter. he points it in front of sebastián's face.)

federico: so that's what you look like.

sebastián: turn that off.

federico: you're beautiful–

sebastián: –don't play with me–

federico: –your skin–

sebastián: –what about it?

federico: it's like coffee. café con leche.

sebastián: what the fuck does that mean?

federico: it was a compliment.

sebastián: stop it.

federico: hasn't anyone ever told you you're beautiful?

(sebastián tries to leave. federico grabs him. they struggle.)

federico: come back with me to my hotel.

sebastián: what the hell do i look like?

federico: when i left my hotel, there was a group of girls looking for dates–

sebastián: why didn't you go with them?

federico: i wasn't interested. i don't even know why they ask.

sebastián: i don't sell myself like that.

federico: how come?

sebastián: i don't know. do i look like the kind of thing people want?

federico: i'd pay you very well–

sebastián: –what for?

federico: you remind me of someone.

sebastián: go back to spain, then.

federico: i overheard someone mentioning there's a guy at my hotel who'll sneak guests in if i bribe him.

sebastián: too risky.

federico: i'll feed you.

sebastián: i'm not that hungry.

(he tries to leave, but federico pulls him towards him.)

sebastián: not on the street.

federico: –now.

(he kisses him. sebastián gives in. but then he breaks away, clutching his mouth.)

sebastián: –you bit me, *carajo–*

federico: –it's been so long since i've kissed someone–

sebastián: –i'm bleeding–

federico: –*ay dios*, i didn't mean to–

sebastián: –what are you trying to do? someone could have seen us.

federico: i'm invisible. i don't exist. no one looks at me, let alone touches me.

(composes himself.)

federico: i'm sorry.

sebastián: i'm sorry means shit.

federico: just tell me your name then i'll leave you alone.

sebastián: *cinco fulas*

federico: five *what?*

sebastián: dollars. the green stuff.

federico: done.

(he offers five dollars. sebastián takes them)

sebastián: sebastián.

federico: *(letting him go.)* thank you, sebastián.

(sebastián runs off.)

2.

(connie's dressing room in la iglesia, a cabaret housed in what used to be a church. the building is a shambles. connie, a woman in her forties stands smoking in her underwear before a statue of la caridad del cobre. *benito, a fair, unassuming young man enters with a dress and a bottle of rum.)*

connie: *(to the statue.)* i know you're up to something, *cachita.* . .

benito: *querida?*

connie: ... don't play *la inocente.* i know you've got it in for me.

benito: the show begins in ten minutes. i've brought you the blue one.

connie: *(to benito.)* bring me the red one.

benito: it's not finished.

connie: *pero que manera de joder, chico! (to statue.)* who'd i fuck over in a past life to deserve this shit?

benito: i had to clean the confessionals today and you know how long it takes when i have to carry the bucket up and down the stairs and down the street and back because that pump is the only–

connie: –not today, benito, not today.

(she begins angrily applying her makeup.)

benito: *(pulling something from his pocket.)* when i was cleaning, i found another one.

connie: *(interested.)* another *estampita?* you'd think we'd have found all of them by now. *(reaching out her hand.)* let's see it.

(benito hands her a small card.)

connie: cute baby.

benito: it's jesus and saint anthony.

connie: *(reading.)* "o, st. anthony! saint of miracles! saint of help! i have need of this special favor." no shit.

benito: he was great with heretics. he said the trick was to repeat the name of mary over and over again when you speak to them.

connie: mary. mary. mary …

benito: you also pray to him when you lose stuff.

connie: how do you know this?

benito: well, it's obvious from looking at the picture, isn't it?

connie: don't get smart with me. add it to the collection.

(connie hands it back to him. benito places it in a box full of other estampitas.)

connie: *(continuing to apply her makeup.)* ay, coño, why do i feel like killing myself?

benito: you need sleep.

connie: i sleep fine.

benito: you had another nightmare.

connie: that's ridiculous. i don't have nightmares. i don't even dream.

benito: i heard you screaming.

connie: i don't scream!!!!

benito: why don't you have a drink?

connie: not today. it'll make my stomach turn.

benito: you always have a little rum–

connie: that's it! i *always* have a little rum. i'm sick of it. sick to death. there are other things worth drinking.

benito: like what?

connie: *(eyes glazing over.)* champagne!

benito: *querida*, you're getting carried away.

connie: carried away? you hear that, *cachita?* he says i'm getting carried away! well, alright, i am. champagne! say it benito. champagne!!! can't you feel the way it sparkles? like crushed glass. i'd give anything to have some. and i almost did. last night i sat myself down with one of the customers. french. and i thought, i bet i can get this *maricón* to buy me a bottle of champagne. and do you know what i did?

benito: no.

connie: i told him i was the cuban piaf.

benito: who?

connie: shush! i asked him, how can i sing songs of love, of heartbreak, of passion without ever having had a drop of something as romantic as champagne? i told him he'd be contributing to the development of a down on her luck latin american talent.

benito: and what did he say?

connie: he pointed somewhere behind me and said, "i want him." he was pointing to miguel or lázaro, i don't know, they all look alike to me. "how much?" "one bottle of champagne," i said. i was scared. i mean miguel has no ass and i've gotten complaints about lázaro's dick, so i knew champagne was overcharging. but he reached into his pocket and gave me forty *fulas.*

benito: forty?

connie: two twenties! i froze. my heart stopped. i even stopped sweating for a second. i thought i'd died. but i took the cash. and like the cuban piaf that i was, *je ne regrette rien*, well almost. i didn't even know if you could get champagne at the diplo store. and i didn't find out. *(she's crying.)* when i went today, some guy grabbed me and dragged me into a side street.

(sebastián appears behind her.)

sebastián: i know you.

connie: i don't think so. i've never seen you in my life.

sebastián: where you going?

connie: what happened to your lip?

sebastián: none of your business.

connie: funny. i was going to say the same to you. goodbye.

(he disappears.)

connie: and then he was gone. and i immediately checked my purse. and the money was gone.

benito: did you check it when you left?

connie: that's ridiculous. no one goes near my purse here *(she's crying.)* … oh, shit, my makeup. this shoe polish ain't cheap. *(she runs to the mirror and tries to salvage her makeup despite her tears.)* his eyes were the blackest i've ever seen. i swear he looked like the devil himself … he … he … he was bleeding.

(benito runs to comfort her.)

benito: *querida*, it's going to be alright.

connie: don't touch me.

benito: i don't want to see you upset.

connie: i can get upset if i feel like it. i don't need taking care of, like someone i know. you owe a lot to me. this job. your bedroom–

benito: *(under his breath.)* –the dirty mattress–

connie: –the only reason you're here is because you couldn't trick for shit and i felt bad for you.

benito: well, i do keep this place up.

connie: yeah, collecting *estampitas!* i'd watch myself because there are plenty of starving fuck-ups out there who'd like to have this kind of situation.

benito: i'm sorry.

connie: i don't want to hear it. just get me that stupid dress before i'm any later than you made me already.

(there is knocking offstage. a voice calls out.)

voice: connie! they're waiting for you.

connie: how many tonight?

voice: full house.

connie: let them wait! let them drink! *(muttering.)* the only way they'd care is if i grew a dick.

(benito holds the dress up for her.)

connie: do i have to?

benito: you know they all love you. they do.

connie: i'll be ugly. that dress makes me look like a tent. look at me! i'm a skeleton! how do those *jineteras* get those hips? i'm not a woman. i'm an ironing board.

benito: just put it on. it'll fit. i promise.

(she steps into it and he zips her up. the dress, although old, looks stunning on her.)

connie: *(looking in the mirror.)* huh … well, it's going to have to do. where'd you score the thread?

benito: a friend.

connie: you're not dipping into the profits are you?

benito: of course not. straight to the cigar box. count it.

connie: after the show. oh, shit! that goddamn show … tell me, benito. tell me it'll go ok.

benito: it will. *(jokingly raising a fist.)* la lucha!

connie: stop that before i throw up.

(blackout. then spotlight on a microphone. connie steps into the spot.)

3.

connie: the music starts and her mind could be a thousand miles away, but the travel restrictions apply in the imagination as well. so, it's the same songs. the same pile of bricks. the same faces in the audience waiting for the miracles they'd buy that night. must be nice, to have that kind of hope. to think $20 will turn some *pepillo* whore into the boy they sat next to in algebra. the one they never said a word to, but they'd stare at enough to count how many times they'd breathe during the lesson … or how about the best friend they'd go drinking with? before they got married and had kids? before they lost their hair and gained several inches around their waists? well, abandon every hope, she wanted to say. it's easy to remember, yes, to pretend those lips are someone else's, but can you really make the substitute into the real thing? *¡hijo, no!* in those matters, she was … well, let's say she was experienced. the substitute is a kind of torture. it only reminds you of what you've lost, but it never lets you have it again.

(sebastián appears. connie stops her number and stares at him.)

connie: what the fuck do you want now?

sebastián: *(astonished.)* my mother used to sing that song.

(he passes out.)

connie: *(crossing herself.)* ¡ay, virgen purisima!

(the lights go out.)

4.

(connie's room. benito drags in the unconscious sebastián.)

connie: lay him on the *chaise.*

benito: the what?

connie: the couch

benito: *(dropping him on the couch.)* he cut his forehead.

connie: like i care.

(she shakes sebastián.)

connie: wake up.

sebastián: what the–?

(benito grabs connie, trying to pull her off sebastián.)

benito: leave him alone for a minute. he's not well.

connie: serves him right, *comemierda desgraciado!*

sebastián: what happened?

connie: you fucking robbed me!!!!

benito: *querida*, someone will hear you.

connie: you stay out of this. *(lowering her voice.)* i want my money.

sebastián: *(feeling his lip.)* am i still bleeding?

benito: your forehead. you had a pretty bad fall.

sebastián: i didn't sleep last night.

connie: now, that that's been cleared up, can we talk about my money?

sebastián: what money?

connie: don't play dumb. where's the forty you took from my purse?

sebastián: listen, *mami*, i would've loved to come across forty bucks, but i didn't take your cash.

(connie lunges for him. benito holds her back.)

connie: *cabrón!*

sebastián: look at this lip. a guy bit me hard. spanish tourist. i got blood all over my shirt, but i also got five dollars. not much, but i *earn* my money.

connie: listen, *muñeco*, i've been around for a while, and if there's one thing i've learned is that the only thing people are good at is screwing other people. you expect me to believe you?

sebastián: why would i come here if i robbed you?

connie: to rob me again, stupid! well, you're out of luck. i'm broke. i've got no more money. just a good for nothing statue over there.

(she grabs la caridad del cobre *and throws her at sebastián.)*

benito: *(dropping onto the floor to pick up statue.) querida!*

connie: leave it, benito.

benito: but you've chipped your statue.

connie: i should have thrown her harder!

(she kicks benito.)

connie: off the floor. come on!

sebastián: hey!

benito: *(to sebastián.)* don't say anything. it'll make it worse.

connie: *(grabbing him by the hair.)* what was that? you know, *estoy hasta el ultimo pelo!* you're supposed to be defending me against this … this … *thief* and there you are on the floor picking up all this useless shit. you're so close to walking the streets like this *guajiro* here and i don't think you'll get many offers for that scrawny ass of yours, *ingrato!*

sebastián: i said hey!

connie: do i care? if i screamed out right now, who would the *comité* believe?

sebastián: oh, you mean the *guajiro* or the hooker?

connie: oh, that's where you're wrong, *muñeco.* i am an entertainer who entertains tourists and therefore stimulates the economy. and if … and i mean if … my wait staff are tipped for certain extra services and pay me a certain percentage to keep the place running, then i am far from deserving to be called a common hooker. of course, you *muñeco*, that's another story. i don't know what kind of tricks you've been turning when you end up beat up like you do. but, with a face like yours i wouldn't blame you for selling yourself.

sebastián: you wouldn't, huh?

connie: well, everyone's doing it these days.

sebastián: then put me to work.

connie: oh, benito, did you hear that?

sebastián: i get offers. the spanish tourist tried to take me back to his hotel.

connie: why didn't you?

sebastián: i didn't trust him.

connie: and you trust me?

sebastián: this place has a reputation.

connie: it's my singing.

sebastián: i need a job.

connie: and i need my money back.

sebastián: then maybe we can make a deal–

connie: –hold it right there–

sebastián: you'll get your money.

connie: you think so? you have no experience.

sebastián: i have plenty of experience

connie: benito, does he look *experienced?* how fast do you think he can make me forty bucks?

benito: i don't know, *querida.* miguel's our best and he only makes about ten on a good night … and those don't happen very often.

connie: you hear that, *muñeco?*

sebastián: my name's sebastián.

connie: sebastián. let's say we make this deal. you have two nights. one to watch. the other to work. if you make me eighty bucks by the end of the second night, you stay and keep ten percent. if not, i report you for theft. pretty simple.

sebastián: eighty?

connie: interest. i saw it in a movie.

sebastián: i don't think i can do that.

connie: i admit, it's a gamble … but there's something about you … you could do very well.

sebastián: do you think i'm good looking?

connie: i don't know. what do you think, benito? is he good looking?

benito: um … he'll do.

connie: the kind of guy you wouldn't stand a chance in hell with, eh, benito?

(silence.)

connie: good, now go and clean something. i expect you back here after my second show.

benito: yes, *querida.*

(he exits.)

connie: i want to ask you a question.

sebastián: can i have a cigarette?

connie: then will you answer?

sebastián: depends.

connie: on what?

sebastián: the question.

connie: here's your cigarette.

(they smoke.)

sebastián: alright, now ask.

connie: why'd you stop me on the street?

sebastián: i don't know.

connie: did you know i worked here?

sebastián: no.

connie: then … ?

sebastián: i thought i knew you. it was my mistake. sorry.

connie: people have a way of "knowing" things around here.

sebastián: come on, do i look like i "know" things?

connie: you look like a lot of things, muñeco.

(pause.)

connie: did you mean what you said? about your mother singing that song?

sebastián: yeah.

connie: where is she?

sebastián: dead.

connie: sorry.

sebastián: well, she may as well be. i don't know where she is. she left me with my grandfolks when i was eight.

connie: and your father?

sebastián: who knows? my mother was a slut and that's putting it nicely.

connie: she's still your mother.

sebastián: yeah, she's still that.

connie: *(to herself.)* she's still that …

sebastián: i want to get to work.

connie: you agree to my terms?

sebastián: do i have a choice?

connie: a choice? i haven't seen one of those for ages.

sebastián: are you done?

connie: don't look at me like that.

sebastián: like what?

connie: i'm actually doing you a favor.

sebastián: a favor? i haven't seen one of those for ages.

connie: get to work.

(he exits and she picks the statue up from the floor.)

connie: *(to statue.)* what the hell are you looking at? don't think you didn't have it coming.

voice: *(offstage. knocking loudly.)* connie, they're waiting.

connie: how many?

voice: full house.

connie: *carajo.*

(she tries to light a cigarette. her matches extinguish quickly. the knocking continues. her manner becomes frenetic. a spotlight on connie. she is onstage again. her hands shake as she turns to face the audience. she opens her mouth, a pre-recorded bolero *drowns her out as the light is extinguished.)*

5.

(federico writing in his book, wandering around havana.)

federico: a postcard of *la coppelia*, famous for its ice cream, but secretly famous for the men eyeing each other, communicating in a language that consisted of looks and implications ... and it was what he began to crave, sebastián. your kiss was an infection and he sought the shadows of havana looking for a cure. he would be struck by these nocturnal landscapes and his desire to write to a friend describing them as one would send a postcard of the eiffel tower if one was in paris. but there are no postcards of these dark pockets and there is no one he could send one to if there were—except for you, sebastián. you appeared to him spilling the evidence of your kiss onto his lapel.

(federico disappears. on another part of the stage, sebastián is seen outside the "confessionals," a maze of walls made out of sheets and shadows where the boys perform their services.)

benito: *(in shadows.)* i think you're crazy.

sebastián: *(startled.)* where are you?

benito: *(stepping out.)* you don't know her. she does terrible things

sebastián: what is this place?

benito: *querida* calls it the confessionals. this is where it happens.

sebastián: it's quiet.

benito: usually is when *querida* is singing.

sebastián: does she always sing the same song?

benito: pretty much.

sebastián: not many people out there.

benito: it's the same every night. we can never fill the twelve seats. but we always tell her the house is full. the boys usually watch so she doesn't feel bad.

sebastián: why aren't you up there then?

benito: i've stopped listening a long time ago.

sebastián: you shouldn't let her treat you like that.

benito: she's right. i'm not good for much.

sebastián: sounds like you keep this place running.

benito: i just clean up and take care of *querida*.

sebastián: just?

benito: just. it's no big deal.

sebastián: so what goes on in the "confessionals"?

benito: you should know.

sebastián: do you watch?

benito: sometimes. i play this game … it's stupid.

sebastián: what is it?

benito: do you really want to know?

sebastián: yeah.

benito: i look at the men who come in here. i try to listen to their voices. figure out where they come from. why they're here.

sebastián: can you tell where i'm from?

benito: definitely oriente. maybe holguín.

sebastián: that's pretty good. and why am i here?

benito: *(stuck.)* …

sebastián: am i that difficult to figure out?

benito: you're here for the same reason everyone comes here. these white sheets. it's like a bunch of movie screens, but all you see on them are shadows. movies full of holes. but who you're looking for in the shadows? *yo que se.*

sebastián: i came here looking for my parents.

(benito doesn't look at sebastián.)

benito: are they in havana?

sebastián: they could be in miami for all i know ... sometimes i follow complete strangers for hours, thinking "maybe?" or "is it?"

benito: why's that?

sebastián: we all have to have parents.

benito: do we?

sebastián: don't you?

benito: *(getting up.)* i've got cleaning to do.

(he walks towards the confessional entrance. he turns around and looks at sebastián.)

benito: come with me.

(sebastián follows him. federico appears in another part of the stage, reading from his book.)

federico: postcard of the *madriguera*, where he was told by the locals to stay clear of at night as it is crawling with *maricones*. and it was. he surrendered to an assault of foreign mouths and hands and cocks piecing them together into a picture of you. before he kissed you – his limbs hung lifeless, corpse-like. his memory, erased every morning. his life, he felt, belonged to someone else. he was a character in a play. not a person. not federico. who was he? he'd repeat the name over and over. federico.

federico. and all he knew was federico was lost in the darkness and his suit was getting dirtier. soon, no one would be able to find him.

(federico disappears, shift to behind the sheets at the confessional.)

sebastián: you believe me, don't you? i didn't take her money.

benito: were you following her?

sebastián: i didn't mean to.

benito: she was scared.

sebastián: do i look scary to you?

benito: your lip.

sebastián: oh, yeah … *that.*

benito: she's nervous–

sebastián: –stop defending her.

benito: i believed you.

sebastián: thanks. so where's the cleaning you had to do?

benito: *(pulling out a handkerchief from his pocket. a piece of paper falls out.)* here.

(he places the handkerchief to sebastián's lip.)

benito: you have some dried blood there still.

sebastián: you dropped something.

benito: where?

sebastián: there. on the ground next to your foot.

(he reaches down and picks it up.)

benito: let me have that.

sebastián: why? what is it?

benito: just give it to me.

sebastián: *(looking at it.)* it's from connie's collection.

benito: it's an *estampita* of san sebastián.

sebastián: it looks like mine.

benito: you have one?

(sebastián pulls one out of his pocket.)

sebastián: i stole it from my grandmother. i always wanted to ask her about him. i mean, he's my *santo*. leave it to me to have a *santo* with all those arrows.

benito: he was executed.

sebastián: what for?

benito: he was a christian and the romans didn't like that. so they tied him up and fired all these arrows into him.

sebastián: he likes it, doesn't he?

benito: *(moistening the handkerchief with his mouth and cleaning up sebastian's lip.)* all *santos* like pain.

sebastián: *(wincing.)* not me.

benito: what was he like? the guy?

sebastián: he wore a white suit … and he looked at me funny.

benito: like how?

sebastián: he said he was scared. he was lost.

benito: how much did he offer you?

sebastián: a lot.

benito: he liked what he saw.

sebastián: seems to be the only thing i've got going for me.

(sebastián kisses benito. the kissing becomes passionate. connie's shadow emerges and looms large behind the sheet. she draws it back.)

connie: excuse me, *muñeco*, but this isn't the sort of training i told you to get. and as for you, benito, i told you i needed you after the second show.

benito: yes, *querida*.

connie: i suppose you've learned all there is to know if you had time to fool around.

sebastián: he was just showing me–

connie: *–no me jodas!* get back out there. remember, i want eighty tomorrow night.

(blackout, then federico is revealed once more.)

federico: postcard of *la iglesia*. a dark building on an even darker street. a private cabaret and supposedly *quite the place*. and just as well. a church is always a fitting reservoir for sin.

6.

(the entrance to la iglesia. federico enters. benito emerges from a shadowy recess.)

benito: nice suit.

federico: *(startled.)* don't!

benito: forgive me, *señor.*

federico: i didn't see you. you scared me.

benito: here to see the show?

federico: is that what they call it?

benito: call what? this is a cabaret, *señor.*

federico: and are you the *maître 'd?*

benito: the what?

federico: i was hoping to get a seat.

benito: sit anywhere you like. i only wanted to ask you. well, sometimes i try to guess where the clients are from–

federico: –spain. so they tell me–

benito: –so they tell you?

federico: it's been so long, i've forgotten it. do you serve drinks?

benito: well, i guessed spain. i was going to tell you that. i've gotten really good at guessing.

federico: i see. how many "clients" have you um … you know.

benito: talked to?

federico: is that what you do? talk to them?

benito: i don't usually talk to anyone.

federico: you don't?

benito: you're the first.

federico: why me?

benito: i know you ... i mean, i know about you.

federico: you do? tell me.

benito: you bite.

federico: sebastián!

benito: he told me you wore a white suit ... well, it's almost white.

(he points to the blood on federico's lapel.)

benito: there he is, isn't he?

federico: you need to tell me. is he here?

benito: you have to arrange it with *querida*. he's very popular ... but offer her eighty and he's yours, i guarantee it. don't tell her i told you this because she hates making it easy for anybody.

federico: and how much does she charge for you?

benito: me? i'm not for sale.

federico: too good for this sort of thing, huh?

(silence.)

federico: you look hungry.

benito: you can't imagine.

(federico pulls out some money.)

benito: save it for sebastián.

federico: so what's in it for you, tipping me off like this?

benito: i like to hear your voice. it reminds me other places exist. even for a second.

(music.)

benito: now, sit, before *querida* gets onstage.

7.

connie: another show. same songs. same story. same game. she scanned the audience, hoping something would be different – and that's when she saw him, wearing the whitest suit she'd ever seen. he looked at her. he scribbled in a book, writing down her every move. and she was ... upset? no, she had no time to be upset. she had to act happy! she had to sing her "cubans-dance-the-mambo-night-and-day" song. she had to think of something else, anything but the man in the suit ... she looked away from him and thought about her collection of *estampitas* ... and she ... begins to list the *santos* in the box in her room: anthony, francis, lucy, bernadette, stephen, theresa, agnes ... agnes.

"forced into prostitution," benito told her. she did not need reminding.

there was a girl who ran in here from the street with a pair of legs, thin like eggshells and covered with rust ... no ... covered with blood. the girl said, "have you seen my mother?" and she told the girl, "no. i haven't seen your mother. i have no idea who she is." she shoved the girl out the door and as soon as she touched the girl, her hands turned to ice ... her hands ...

(she stares at her hands.)

applause. the song was over. and he was still staring at her.

8.

(sebastián watching connie's performance he is smoking.)

benito: *(from the shadows.)* where'd you get the smokes?

sebastián: first customer. he gave me eight *fulas* and a pack of camels.

benito: i'm sorry about what happened in the confessionals.

sebastián: forget it.

benito: why?

sebastián: shit like that happens.

(he offers benito a cigarette.)

sebastián: friends?

(benito takes a cigarette and smells it.)

benito: i've never smoked a camel.

sebastián: you *can* smoke, can you? wouldn't want to waste a cigarette.

benito: smoking kills your appetite. it's a useful skill.

(they smoke.)

sebastián: i don't know if this deal with connie is going to work out.

benito: she'll get her money back. you've already made eight.

sebastián: it's too many *fulas* to make in one night.

benito: what if i told you that you don't really have to worry about making that money?

sebastián: well … i only made eight with the last guy. i don't think i'll get ten more of those.

(music stops. connie's act is over. the lights brighten.)

sebastián: shit, she's done. i need to get out there.

(he scans the room. connie walks over to federico's table.)

connie: don't think i didn't see you.

federico: see me what?

sebastián: *(seeing federico.)* ay, coño.

benito: what's wrong?

sebastián: it's him. i can't go out there.

benito: do it! he'll pay the eighty.

sebastián: i don't care if he'll give me eight hundred.

benito: but … you see, i've arranged it.

sebastián: you've what?

benito: you wouldn't have made your money any other way.

sebastián: who the hell do you think you are? my pimp?

benito: you don't hear those men every night. bragging how low they were able to talk down the price.

sebastián: i don't need you taking care of me.

benito: go fuck yourself, then–

(sebastián physically threatens benito. silence. sebastián retreats.)

sebastián: benito?

benito: i've got sewing to finish. and i have to count the money. so bring me whatever else you make before you go to bed ... *if* you make anything else.

(he leaves. the scene shifts back to connie and federico.)
connie: you with that pencil. with that notebook. anything wrong with my singing?

federico: not a thing. i just wanted to remember you.

connie: most people take a picture.

federico: well, this is the way i do it.

connie: *(grabbing federico's book. reading.)* she scanned the audience, hoping something would be different. and that's when she saw him. wearing the whitest suit she's ever seen. he looked at her. he scribbled in a book. and then it happened. the white of his pages, of his clothes, spilling out her thoughts like a box of old photographs.

(she drops the book.)

federico: you don't like it?

connie: i don't like people ... *writing* during my act, *señor*.

federico: i wanted to remember–

connie: –so you said–

federico: –remember myself. what i was doing. you made me remember something. and i wanted a picture of me remembering.

connie: that's impossible.

federico: why?

connie: because you're taking the picture ... i mean, writing ... whatever.

federico: that's why i'm never "i"", but rather "he." someone i don't know. someone i don't remember.

connie: you, *señor*, are drunk!

federico: not at all.
connie: the name's connie–

federico: just connie?

connie: just.

(she sits down.)

federico: that's an unusual stage name. it is a stage name?

connie: why is it unusual?

federico: it's english.

connie: i like it. it's very me, don't you think? i like english. it's clear. it's cold.

federico: well, i've never met a connie … not that i remember anyway.

connie: so, tell me. so what else are you trying to remember?

federico: i have a feeling i should ask you that very question.

connie: me? i'm too busy trying to forget … just like you it seems.

federico: i've got money i'm willing to spend. i suggest we change the subject before i change my mind.

connie: *(cool. she only betrays her excitement in the way she lights another cigarette.)* no te pongas asi, mi amor. we were only having a civilized conversation. we do have them on this island, no matter what they tell you in spain. if you'd like to talk business, i'd be more than happy to, but … it isn't that often someone comes in here and *writes* … it isn't that often anyone is inspired to do anything but sleep or drink during my act–

federico: –i want sebastián.

(pause.)

connie: you know him?

federico: why do you ask?

connie: he's new.

federico: i've seen him around.

(she points to the blood on federico's suit.)

connie: i can see that.

federico: he bit me.

connie: really? he came in here looking for a job ... petrified ... lip a little swollen ... because some guy bit *him*.

federico: he lied.

connie: must have been some bite to draw blood like that. sebastián's lip's still a little swollen. yours looks fine to me. but, then again, you can buy all sorts of ointments at the diplo store. probably things most of us have never heard of.

(federico pulls out $80.)

federico: thank god for the diplo store. there's quite a bit you can buy there.

connie: champagne? can you buy champagne?

federico: well, i'm sure you could. i never–

connie: –i've always had this fantasy–

federico: –that's a pretty outlandish fantasy–

connie: –just because we're third world doesn't mean we don't have goals.

federico: but champagne?

connie: i could say the same about sebastián.

federico: that's ridiculous.

connie: you're giving me eighty *fulas* for him.

federico: isn't that what he goes for?

connie: i don't know. who told you that?

(sebastián appears.)

sebastián: lázaro did. *(to federico.)* didn't you ask him about me?

federico: yes … i did.

connie: sebastián, i take it you know *señor … señor …*

federico: federico.

sebastián: yeah. an old friend of mine. i was in the confessionals when he came in, so he asked lázaro.

connie: yeah, i'm sure.

sebastián: i told him that's what you were asking for me. was i not supposed to?

connie: isn't he the one who bit you?

sebastián: no, that was someone else. this one likes to be bitten.

connie: i want one hundred for him.

sebastián: a hundred?

connie: it's insurance

federico: what for?

connie: in case you break him.

federico: one hundred it is.

(he whips out a hundred dollars and tosses them on the table.)

federico: have fun at the diplo store.

(she stares at the money. benito appears behind her.)

benito: he did it. he did better than you thought.

connie: what are you doing here?

(he hands her the red dress.)

benito: it's finished. better get out of that one. it needs a wash.

connie: a hundred dollars! i'm hiding this in a safe place.

benito: i'll wait for you in your room.

connie: benito … ?

(he's gone..)

9.

(the confessionals. federico and sebastián are seen.)

federico: you don't look too happy.

sebastián: fuck off.

federico: smoke?

sebastián: i got my own.

federico: resourceful.

(they light up.)
federico: why don't you like me?

sebastián: i'm just doing my job. i don't have to like you.

federico: you act as if i've done something terrible to you.

sebastián: well, it's not like you've been doing me any favors.

federico: i just paid 100 for you. i could have gotten someone else for a tenth of that.

sebastián: well, let's get started. wouldn't want you to waste a cent.

(he grabs federico's face and begins kissing him. federico struggles.)

federico: not like that.

sebastián: how then?

federico: don't you think 100 lets me kiss the way i want?

sebastián: make it quick, then

federico: what? you have a waiting list?

sebastián: what the fuck is it to you?

federico: how come you wouldn't go with me a couple nights ago and now i find you working here?

sebastián: you gave me the idea. i thought i might be worth something.

federico: i only offered you money because i didn't think you'd go with me otherwise.

sebastián: i've never been that picky.

federico: then why didn't you–?

sebastián: there was something wrong with you.

federico: why's that?

sebastián: no one's ever thought much of me.

federico: well, connie must think the world of you. 100!

sebastián: she thinks i robbed her.

federico: you look like a thief.

sebastián: what do you know about how i look?

federico: the way you're standing there with that cigarette …

(sebastián stands against the sheet. he becomes a giant shadow.)

sebastián: is this the way a thief stands?

federico: actually, yes …

sebastián: how do you know?

federico: i saw one just like that on *calle de san marcos*–

sebastián: –where?

federico: madrid.

sebastián: how'd you know he was he a thief?

federico: he looked dangerous.

sebastián: do i look dangerous?

federico: extremely.

(federico kisses sebastián.)

sebastián: take off your jacket.

federico: what?

sebastián: i want to see it.

(federico takes off his jacket and hands it to sebastián, taking his book out of his pocket before doing so.)

sebastián: what's in the book?

federico: you just asked for the jacket. not the book.

(sebastián puts on the jacket.)

sebastián: it doesn't fit.

federico: you look like a little boy.

sebastián: so, i'm not dangerous anymore?

(federico shakes his head. he rubs his hands through sebastián's hair. sebastián softens somewhat.)

federico: why does connie think you robbed her?

sebastián: i stopped her on the street she looked ... no, she *walked*, trying to sway her hips, but it was like she'd broken something. and she reminded me ... well, my mother used to walk like that and i'm not much fun when i remember her. so i must have scared her or something.

federico: what was your father like?

sebastián: who knows? my mother said he died. my mother said sometimes he came to her in her sleep ... she said ... she said he was dressed in white–

federico: –a white suit?

sebastián: he was an angel, she said. and i believed her at the time. my father was an angel … or a ghost … *yo que se* … but he was dead or arrested or something. so, that was her excuse. no reason why he'd gone. so i used to make up reasons. he was a spy … a counterrevolutionary … a thinker … a writer … that was my favorite. it was the furthest thing from holguín that i could come up with–

federico: –is that where you're from?–

sebastián: –my father wasn't dead. she was a slut. he could have been anyone. but when i saw you … your white suit. oh, man, i thought she was right. *mi puta madre* was right … and there you were … and you wanted me …

(he reaches out and touches federico on the shoulder.)

sebastián: but you're not a ghost.

federico: *(stepping away.)* yes, i am. look in the breast pocket.

sebastián: what's in here?

(sebastián takes out a photograph.)

federico: "a picture of federico in havana. 'if i were ever to become lost, they can find me here.'" for a long time, it was the only thing i could remember.

sebastián: he's wearing a white suit, too … *(he looks at federico.) hombre,* this picture's like seventy years old.

federico: i found it in the suit.

sebastián: where'd you find that?

federico: madrid.

sebastián: with the thief?

(silence.)

sebastián: what's wrong?

federico: he wasn't a thief. just a boy. just like most of the other boys running around *chueca*. he came up to me on the street and kissed me. i knew those kisses had a price tag attached. but that didn't stop me from inviting him to my hotel. and i watched him undress. his body stood out against the curtains i drew over the windows. and as i moved closer, i saw his skin was really a pale sky, covered with a galaxy of moles–

sebastián: and then what happened?

(pause.)

federico: i don't know. i woke up after god knows how many days. i was bruised. in pain. there was a large bandage around my middle, covering a gash in my side… and i couldn't remember anything. not even my name. i phoned the front desk. i had been attacked. my wallet stolen. but the manager assured me i had left most of my cash in a safety deposit box downstairs. quite a bit of cash. and a passport. this suit was in the closet. and that picture. "federico in havana." it matched the name on the passport. and i was lost. no one had come to claim me in madrid, so i came here. i kept this suit as white as i could. i wanted to be found.

sebastián: and i found you. is that what you're trying to say?

federico: after i met you, i started to remember snatches of things. so i started to write them down in this book … *(pause.)* i had memories. postcards of things that actually happened. not stories i made up about a man named federico.

sebastián: the guy in the picture?

federico: no. he's a writer. famous … and dead. i have been a different federico, entirely.

sebastián: so why him?

federico: there was something about his face … he *was* lost.

sebastián: *(handing the photograph back to federico.)* here.

federico: *(putting it back in his book.)* thank you.

(sebastián kisses federico the kissing intensifies as the scene fades to …)

10.

(… connie undressing. benito unzips her dress and she sits at her table. she places the $100 in her purse. benito brings her a basin with water.)

connie: set it here.

(he places it in on the table in front of her. she dunks her face in. silence. benito stands behind her. she suddenly comes up for air, gasping.)

connie: towel!

(he hands it to her. she rubs the makeup off her face. benito takes the basin away.)

connie: that water tastes like rust.

(like clockwork, benito returns with a drink.)

benito: this will kill the taste.

connie: one last little rum before i buy the bubbly tomorrow.

benito: you talk like you've had it before.

connie: *que va, chico.* i may know about a lot of things, but about champagne? fantasies!

(she lights a cigarette.)

connie: i knew a man once who promised me all the champagne i could drink. they always do.

benito: who was he?

connie: why do you want to know?

benito: just curious.

connie: just a tourist. same shit. they tease us with visions of other places and leave without telling us how to get there. but you wouldn't have any idea about that, i suppose. i guess if one of them ever looked at you. kissed you, so you could just taste everything they promise you ... but you're not that ambitious, are you?

benito: sorry?

connie: i know you like him.

benito: the kind of guy i wouldn't stand a chance in hell with.

(silence.)

connie: i wouldn't get too excited. i'm sure he's gotten used to the idea of sleeping with unattractive people to get what he wants.

benito: do you need anything else or can i go?

(she grabs him.)

connie: you arranged the whole thing with the white suit, didn't you?

benito: what if i did?

connie: you have no experience dealing with clients. you don't know what kind of man he is.

benito: well, he gave you the money. what do you care?

connie: you need to listen to me. if you're going to have the misfortune of falling in love with men, you should know a little more about them.

benito: i've been around here enough.

connie: a man can use you as easily as his toothbrush. you hear me?

benito: perfectly.

connie: did you talk to him?

benito: just a little.

connie: he wrote during my act. and he said the weirdest thing to me. "i wanted to take a picture of myself remembering." *(she stops.)*

benito: what's wrong?

connie: pour me another drink … my hands …

(she rubs her hands nervously as he pours. he puts the glass in her hands. silence.)

connie: i can't feel it.

(benito takes the glass and puts it to her mouth. she drinks.)

benito: you're tired.

connie: i don't feel well.

(he sets down the glass and collects the soiled towel and connie's purse.)

connie: will you check up on the boys before the lights go out and then come back here, please?

benito: yes, *querida.*

connie: i really need you here tonight.

benito: yes, *querida.*

connie: i never understood why you call me that.

benito: *(pause.)* me neither.

(he exits as the scene fades to …)

11.

(the confessionals. federico is on top of sebastián, kissing him. their clothes are in a state of removal. suddenly, federico stops.)

sebastián: what's wrong?

(federico raises himself. we see his bandage. there is blood all over him.)

federico: i'm bleeding.

(he checks the bandage and then notices sebastián.)

federico: it's you!

sebastián: *hombre,* that's impossible. this is your blood.

federico: there's a gash at your side. right where that boy … *ay, dios!*

sebastián: you just bled on me, that's all. we'll clean you up. stay.

federico: i feel sick.

sebastián: *(pulling federico back on top of him.)* just lay here with me. relax …

federico: i want to forget.

sebastián: what do you want to forget, *papi?*

(the word makes federico tense up more.)

federico: everything.

(he gets up, grabs sebastián's shirt and tries to wipe the blood.)

federico: we've got to clean up. we've got to get everything like it never happened. and then i'll ask connie for my money.

sebastián: you can't.

federico: i barely touched you.

sebastián: she'll throw me out.

federico: that's of no concern to me. i have to get out of here. you've made me remember something i shouldn't–

sebastián: –what? what did i remind you of?

federico: i should ask you that. that's why you stopped me on the street. to torment me. i'm not your father, sebastián.

sebastián: and i'm not that guy in madrid.

(silence.)

sebastián: you wanna tell me what really happened?

federico: what really happened is none of your business.

sebastián: of course it is. i'm the thief. i'm the dangerous one. i'm the one you cut. the one you bit. you made me bleed.

(he grabs federico by the throat.)

sebastián: is this how it happened?

federico: let me go.

sebastián: you were on top of him. devouring him. smothering him.

federico: no, i never did–

sebastián: *(throwing federico to the ground.)* –you wanted to make me disappear. like my mother. like my father. like i never lived.

federico: how could i make you disappear? all i wanted was to see your face. to know your name. to remember you.

sebastián: no, not me. i'm just a note in your book. *el guajiro caliente,* that's all. so why don't you just go fuck another one. this island's full of them.

federico: i might get a better deal.

sebastián: how much do you think i'm worth, then? 20 *fulas?* 10? 3?

federico: *(opening the book.)* how much did you say? 3?

(he rips out some pages and throws them to sebastián.)

sebastián: what are you doing?

federico: not enough? how about 3 more? i'm afraid this is the only currency i have.

(sebastián picks up the pages.)

sebastián: *(looking at the pages.)* what did you write here?

federico: figure it out.

sebastián: read them to me!

federico: aren't you a little too big to be read to?

(federico tries to leave. benito appears behind him.)

benito: *señor,* what's going on?

sebastián: benito, help me.

benito: *(noticing sebastián.)* what happened to you?

federico: let me pass. i need to speak to connie–

benito: *(holding federico.)* explain to me what happened. *querida* won't make it easy for any of us if there's trouble!

connie: *(offstage.)* benito!

benito: she'll be down here soon.

federico: *(to benito.)* let me through, please.

benito: *señor*, please–

connie: *(off.)* benito!

federico: i need to speak to her.

(the scene freezes.)

12.

(connie appears. she is on the other side of the sheet, making her way to where benito, sebastián, and federico are.)

connie: before she knew it the lights had gone out and the darkness had come. how much time had passed since benito had left her alone? would benito ever come back? would he leave her to breathe this black air, defenseless? she made her way to the confessionals realizing the darkness was not around her, but in front of her on the white sheet, suffocated with shadow. she needed to get through it. past it. behind it. she reached out her hand …

(she pulls aside the sheet, revealing the prior scene, which resumes with her entrance.)

connie: benito? where have you been? it's dark. i thought i asked you to come to me.

federico: i want a refund.

connie: *(suddenly snapping out of it.)* refund? *señor*, you weren't satisfied?

federico: i'm afraid not.

(connie notices the blood.)

connie: benito, *que coño es esto?* what happened here? someone???

(silence.)

sebastián: *(in a trance.)* if i were ever to become lost, they can find me here.

connie: *perdón?*

sebastián: *(beginning to shake.)* if i were ever to become lost, they can find me here.

federico: *(to sebastián.)* you tell her what happened!

connie: why don't you tell me yourself?

federico: what the hell is all of this? i paid you a hundred!

(sebastián shakes violently. benito rushes out to hold him.)

sebastián: if i were ever to become lost, they can find me here.

benito: he's bleeding!

connie: *señor,* what have you done to him?

federico: i should ask you – what has he done to me?

(he raises his shirt to reveal his bloody bandage.)

federico: don't you think this entitles me to a refund?

connie: this is trouble and i don't like trouble. i'm going to make this easy. instead of a refund, i will give you a head start, which is much more valuable. i can raise *un escandalo* so big, you wish you never came here.

federico: i'll be back tomorrow.

connie: if you can remember.

(federico leaves. connie runs over to sebastián, who is lying limp in benito's arms.)

connie: put him on the ground. *(she feels around his chest.)* i can't find the wound.

(blackout.)

13.

(later in the confessionals. connie is wiping the blood of sebastián and pressing a damp rag to his head. sebastián is feverish.)

sebastián: when i was a kid, i had a lot of fevers.

connie: you had something worse than that last night.

sebastián: my mother used to sit and hold a wash towel to my head. she wouldn't move until the fever broke. until then, she sang to me.

connie: yes, we all know she had quite a repertoire. what did she sing? lullabies?

sebastián: sometimes. other times she sang *boleros*. or elvis presley. and then there were other songs. i never heard those before. songs about angels and jesus and mary and stuff. i thought she was making them up, so i asked her about them. she said the fever must have given me dreams. she didn't care much for jesus, who she called a *maricón desgraciado*. a lot of good jesus did her, she said. but i think she was lying.

connie: i think she was right. you were feverish. you hallucinated. it happens.

sebastián: how the fuck do you know? were you there?

connie: you're not the first kid with a fever i've taken care of, *muñeco.*

sebastián: yeah, well, aren't you the lucky one?

connie: more than you know. so. you want to tell me what the hell happened with the white suit?

sebastián: something happened?

connie: *no te hagas el bobo.* we could get into some serious shit if he twists the story around. there was blood all over you, but no wound.

sebastián: i don't remember.

connie: he's got a bandage. he could say you did it to him.

sebastián: he's not going to say anything.

connie: how do you know?

sebastián: what's he going to say? i was going to fuck this guy and he stabbed me?

connie: that's true. but still ...

(she pulls out a knife, which she runs along sebastián's side, while holding her hand over his mouth. he bleeds.)

sebastián: why ... ?

connie: i just wanna be safe.

sebastián: you fucking bitch!

connie: it's for your own good.

sebastián: no, for *your* own good.

(he grabs some of federico's pages and presses them to his wound.)

connie: don't do that. let benito clean it up so it won't get infected.

sebastián: you think i'm going to trust either one of you?

connie: i know what i'm doing.

sebastián: oh, yeah. you know exactly what the fuck you're doing! always full of bright ideas. is that what you think about when you sing?

connie: what do you think about when you steal?

sebastián: what do you think about when you're drunk?

connie: did you think about your mother last night when you were with the white suit?

sebastián: were you thinking about your kid?

(silence.)

sebastián: that's it, isn't it, mami? i knew there was a reason you reminded me.

connie: you really think you know a lot, don't you?

sebastián: what's to know? a bitch mother is a bitch mother.

connie: *(turning to leave.)* i'll send benito over to take care of you.

sebastián: *(stumbling over to her.)* was it a boy or a girl?

connie: benito!

sebastián: *(pressing his body up against her.)* how old was it? *mami?*

connie: what the hell do you think this is? you're nothing to me. just smoke.

sebastián: *(to connie.)* just smoke, huh?

(sebastián kisses her. they embrace. sebastián pushes connie away. she is weeping and bloody.)

connie: get out.

sebastián: i want my cut from last night.

connie: *(grabbing the knife from the floor.)* gladly.

benito: *(entering.) querida!*

(he runs over to her and restrains her.)

connie: let me go, *carajo!*

benito: get out, sebastián. leave!

sebastián: you owe me, *mami.*

(he exits. connie drops the knife and grabs onto benito, tightly.)

connie: the money.

benito: it's in your purse.

connie: run and get it. bring it here. we're going to count it and then you're taking that money and going to the diplo store. i want all the champagne you can get.

(the lights fade.)

14.

(one week later. connie standing in her slip, looking in the mirror, much like the beginning of the play. benito comes in holding out a red dress.)

benito: *querida?* the show begins in ten minutes. i brought you the red one.

connie: where's the blue one?

benito: it needs mending.

connie: what does?

benito: the hem.

connie: i hate the red dress.

benito: i thought the red was your favorite.

connie: it makes me look like *una qualquiera*.

benito: it'll have to be the red one tonight. i can't get the blue one fixed right now.

connie: why not?

benito: i haven't slept for days. i've sat next to your bed for a week now.

connie: *(jumping.)* did you hear that?

benito: you're barely sleeping yourself.

connie: shh! *(silence. they listen ...)* nothing. did you go to the diplo store?

benito: yes.

connie: and?

benito: no champagne. they told me to check again tomorrow.

connie: fucking diplo store.

(loud knock at the door.)

voice: connie, there's someone at the door for you.

connie: benito, go see who it is and tell them to fuck off. i'm in no mood.

benito: yes, *querida*.

(he exits and reappears in another part of the stage, where a disheveled federico is waiting. over the following, connie puts on her dress and her lipstick and pours herself a glass of rum.)

benito: you know you shouldn't be here.

federico: where is he?

benito: we haven't seen him in a week, *señor*.

federico: he's been following me. coming out of the lobby of my hotel. walking down the *malecón*. i can't sleep. the minute i close my eyes, i hear him. breathing. i swear he's in the room with me.

(sebastián appears in connie's room. connie sees him in her mirror. he is holding a knife. connie is nervous, yet very still.)

sebastián: when the soldiers caught sebastián they asked him, "sebastián, do you believe in god? do you believe you're beautiful? do you believe you'll be alive tomorrow? do you believe your mother loved you?" and sebastián answered every question "yes." and every time he did, they shot him until his body disappeared.

(connie turns around to face him. he has vanished. connie grabs the box of estampitas and begins searching:)

connie: *(as the following scene between federico and benito unfolds.)* lucy, francis, anthony, martin ... sebastián. *(she rips it up.)* theresa, barbara ... where is she? agnes? *(looking feverishly.)* lázarus, ignatius, sebastián. *(she rips it up.)* where's agnes? agnes? *(looking some more.)* sebastián!

(she begins ripping them all up.)

benito: leave your hotel. leave the country.

federico: i've lost my plane ticket. i'm running out of cash. and i don't know if i'll be getting any more.

benito: why not?

federico: because that's up to my wife. i left her two weeks ago. just left her and my son. i emptied out our checking account and checked into a hotel in madrid. do you think … do you think connie would give me that money back if i asked her? i can't stay here.

benito: where would you go?

federico: i don't know … somewhere else. i can't live here. i don't know who can. it's an island of skeletons. the buildings have leprosy.

benito: i have your money.

federico: where?

benito: hidden. i'll give it back to you if you help me. take me with you.

federico: i can't even help myself.

benito: don't you want your money?

federico: not like that. you don't want anything to do with me.

(he leaves. benito runs to connie's room. he finds her slumped over in her chair. he grabs her and tries to lift her up.)

benito: *querida*, get up … the show …

connie: i can't sing.

benito: you have to.

connie: *(rubbing her hands.)* benito, it's happening again.

benito: *(grabbing her hands.)* they're like ice.

connie: it's going up my arms

benito: —it'll pass, *querida*—

connie: *(shoving him.)* —no, it won't.
benito: you're just nervous.

connie: nervous doesn't even begin to describe this shit.

benito: —i take care of you.

connie: i can take care of myself.

benito: can you? *(holding out the dress.)* let's get you dressed

connie: *(as she steps into the dress and gets zipped up.)* i want you to search the building.

benito: again?

connie: i don't trust him.

benito: he's not here.

connie: you know what i think? i think you're hiding him in here. do you two *maricones* think you can sit and have a laugh at my expense?

benito: of course not.

connie: i'd love to believe that.

(she turns to leave. she stops.)

connie: who was that at the door by the way?

benito: the man in the white suit. he says he's going to place a complaint. excuse me.

(he storms out past her.)

15.

(benito enters the confessionals. a match is lit and soon a cigarette can be seen.)

sebastián: want a smoke?

benito: keep it.

sebastián: they're camels …

benito: the white suit's seen you.

sebastián: that's impossible.

benito: whatever you're doing, it's got to stop. querida's nerves are shot and i'm not sleeping

sebastián: didn't you miss me?

benito: no.

sebastián: i thought you liked me.

benito: i felt bad for you.

sebastián: that's funny. you feeling bad for me.

benito: isn't that what you wanted coming in here bleeding, begging for a job?

sebastián: and what is it you want mopping the floors, cleaning up her shit?

benito: this isn't about me.

sebastián: no, it's never about you. what does benito need?

benito: i'm fine.

sebastián: is that why you carry him in your pocket? there he is ... all naked. beautiful body. every muscle with an arrow on it and the more pain he feels the better he looks, right? that's what you want.

benito: it's just a pretty picture.

sebastián: that picture has my name.

benito: so that makes you a saint? what the hell have you done? you're not the only orphan or whore on this island.

(connie's singing permeates the walls. they listen to her sing.)

sebastián: it's that song again. it's the one my mother used to sing. she took me to the beach when i was ... two? three? and she'd just sing. she'd sing the entire time. she'd keep singing as she walked into the water ... she was holding me. *(a beat.)* holding me. and she kept on walking until my head was under water.

benito: *(is he being manipulated? does he want to hear this?)* –don't–

sebastián: –everything got dark and i just floated with my eyes closed like i had fallen asleep listening to her voice. when i opened my eyes, i was back on the beach ... alone. my mother gone. just like yours.

benito: how did you know?

sebastián: the other day behind the sheet in the confessionals. i saw you. i saw you and you saw me and we both knew. didn't we? we're the same. isn't that why you kissed me?

(benito shakes his head.)

sebastián: kiss me again?

benito: no.

sebastián: *(advancing.)* –there's nothing to be afraid of, benito. it's just one kiss.

benito: we're *not* the same! everyone wants you! no one wants me! no one!

(sebastián grabs benito. they kiss. sebastián latches onto benito, who struggles to break free. he finally does. there's blood trickling from his lip.)

benito: you bit me, *cara*jo–

sebastián: –that's what it feels like. that's what it feels like to be wanted. you thought know me so well, *compadre.*

benito: it's not so hard. you're practically transparent!

sebastián: good. maybe i can be ignored just like you. maybe i can be numb just like connie. maybe i can forget everything just like the white suit. i think that's fair, isn't it?

(he runs out. benito crumples. connie's shadow appears behind one of the sheets.)

connie: benito?

16.

(connie stumbles in, shaken. benito hides.)

connie: benito, i need you to walk me to bed. i'm so cold … it made it … difficult tonight. my voice just disappeared. and my thoughts … is he with you? are you hiding him? don't do this to me. don't hide from me …

(she grabs one of the sheets hanging from the ceiling and pulls on it. it comes loose.)

connie: benito!

(she begins ripping sheets out, until the entire space is revealed. benito is seen crouching in the corner.)

connie: where is he?

benito: gone.

connie: so he was here?

benito: he just left.

connie: you let him in?

benito: no, of course not.

connie: you've gone behind my back before and if i find out you're helping that thief–

benito: –he never stole your money.

connie: don't protect him.

benito: i took it.

connie: *you?*

benito: surprise.

connie: you lied to me. you've been living it up at my expense!

benito: look at me. do you think i look like i'm living it up in this place?

connie: *no me jodas.* you've got a good thing here.

benito: yeah and your rum comes out the bathroom faucet and all our food comes out of the ration booklet.

connie: i'm not stupid. i know how much things cost. and i also know we make enough to be able to keep this place running.

benito: do we? this place is a dump. why would someone come in here and screw when they can easily grab someone off the street and rent a room? they'll be shutting the whorehouses down when they stop seeing the *fulas.*

connie: don't call this a–

benito: –a whorehouse? what the hell do you think those *desgraciados* come in here for? because they want to hear you sing? we never fill the seats!

connie: don't exaggerate.

benito: me, exaggerate? when you pull your hair out to use for thread, you forget what exaggerating is! let me show you the stitching if you don't believe me.

connie: so what do you want me to do? cry and beat my breast and tell you how fucking scared i am? that i'd fall apart if you left? is that what you want to hear?

(silence.)

connie: i know better than that. i bet you the first guy i see on the street can do this job as good as you.

benito: good. i'm sure he won't mind staying up while you sleep to hold your hand when you wake up screaming.

connie: that's not true.

benito: i've sat in that chair by your bed for a week now. i've watched you sleep. i've watched you twist inside your sheets. what were you dreaming about?

connie: nothing.

benito: what scares you so much?

connie: why do you want to know?

benito: because i'm tired of filling in the blanks. i can't remember my mother. what she was like. or even when she left me. i just want her to have a face.

connie: you want a face? go across the street from the *montserrate* and watch the women looking at the young girls selling themselves. look at them asking themselves how they could ever let their daughters do that sort of thing? if you want something younger, look at the young girls and i'm sure it won't be hard to tell which ones have dumped a baby somewhere so they can turn a few tricks to make ends meet. you can take your pick, benito. but, not me, got it? i don't stand around the *montserrate* anymore.

benito: but you so look the part.

connie: well, good. i guess i'm doomed to play the villain. just leave after you've saved the world, please.

benito: it's not funny.

connie: you might as well. the white suit will place a complaint. we'll be closing soon.

benito: what if i give him the money?

connie: would you really do that?

benito: *(moving towards the door).* i'll see what i can do.

connie: and then when will you be back?

benito: –that i don't know about.

(he exits.)

17.

federico: dear sebastián. one last postcard. *el cayito* by moonlight. a sliver of sand meeting the sea which glows blue even at this time of night. he stands looking at a photograph. not the one he had in his pocket. but one he found in pieces in the sand. he put it together to reveal a picture of what he thought was a family–a mother, a father, and a son whose face was torn in two. and he wondered who had ripped up this picture. this postcard of such a different landscape. and as dark as it was, he could still see their faces–

benito: federico!

(federico disappears and sebastián is standing alone looking at the water.)

sebastián: he's not here.

benito: *(startled).* sebastián?

sebastián: why were you looking for him?

benito: i don't have to tell you.

sebastián: there's nobody here. there were a few guys groping around earlier but–

benito: –what are you doing here, then?

sebastián: there's no moon tonight. i don't know if i like that or not.

benito: i can hardly see you.

sebastián: i'm transparent … i'm smoke.

(he pulls out folded pieces of paper from his pocket.)

sebastián: can you see these?

benito: what are they?

sebastián: postcards from federico. put them in your pocket with your saint.

(silence.)

benito: sebastián–

sebastián: shh … can you hear that?

(silence.)

benito: i can't hear anything.

sebastián: i've been listening all night. for her. her singing. i want her to hold me again. in the dark, under the waves.

benito: there's no one.

(silence.)

benito: how about i make you an offer? i've got the hundred federico paid for you. i'll give it to you if you come with me.

sebastián: i'm not interested anymore.

benito: why not?

sebastián: this island is full of orphans. it doesn't need me.

benito: but i do.

sebastián: no, you don't. i'm the one who needs you.

benito: for what?

sebastián: i need you to read to me.

benito: read to you?

sebastián: just do it.

benito: these pages you gave me?

sebastián: just pick one.

(benito pulls them out and reads.)

benito: he had this dream last night. you were standing by the window in his hotel room in madrid. and you wanted to open the curtains to see the sky. you wanted to open the window to feel the air. and he couldn't understand why you'd want something so cold and black as the sky in madrid, sebastián–

sebastián: *(to himself.)* –cold, black sky …

benito: –opening the window, you caught your finger and pressed it to your lips. and i … i mean *he* … thought how much you looked like his little boy all over again. and he couldn't bear to look at you. so much like his face … my face … and i just wanted to cover your eyes. your mouth. make you turn towards the dark sky you wanted so it would swallow you. but it swallowed me instead. it swallowed me instead.

(he stops. sebastián has disappeared.)

sebastián … ?

(there is no answer, just the sound of the ocean. he stands alone, clutching the pages as the darkness engulfs him. end of play.)

expat/inferno
a play by alejandro morales

developed at new dramatists, intar new works lab, the public theater new work now, dixon place experiments and disorders and produced by packawallop productions at 2003 new york international fringe festival– "overall achievement" award.

characters:

danny: late twenties. latino. oscillates between a very pure vulnerability and a stormy countenance, which he thinks is sexy. he is determined or wants to be.

beatrice: late twenties/early thirties. a presence manifested in two characters: a glamorous french woman living in new york–part louise brooks part edith piaf–and a distraught, yet fabulous, american woman living in paris, rings under her eyes, run down and an expert at the art of suffering.

x: late 30s. danny's ex-boyfriend. is he smart and sophisticated or lost and freaking out? the way we see him depends on how danny remembers him. either way, he is idealized, beautiful and perfect regardless of how together or apart he comes across.

magda: early 50s, latina. almost biblical in her maternal instinct. she is a woman who exudes warmth, despite the fact that she feels everything is getting colder around her.

kenny: late 20s. fair. very beautiful in a cherubic way. he stutters, which often renders him adorably childlike.

go-go garçon: a go-go boy, concierge, bookstore attendant. should be played by the same actor. always menacing.

setting:

new york city and paris, autumn 2001

expat/inferno received its world premiere at the new york international fringe festival, presented by packawallop productions, august 2003. the production was directed by scott ebersold.

cast:

danny	drew cortese
beatrice	polly lee
x	mark h. dold
magda	judith delgado
kenny	nathan m. white
go-go garçon	jason griffin

sets	jo winiarksi
lighting	greg emetaz
costumes	jessica watters
sound	nathan lively
stage mangement	tarah grant

1.

(danny and x, looking at each other.)

x: you are dreaming, danny boy.

danny: what happens in this dream?

x: we are in a bar. we are slightly drunk. in front of us is a stage with a microphone. a woman doing a bad impersonation of a french chanteuse steps on stage and sings *"ne me quitte pas"* by jacques brel.

(beatrice appears singing "ne me quitte pas." *she wears a red dress. her performance is abstracted in some way so she merely provides underscoring to the following:)*

beatrice: *ne me quitte pas*
il faut oublier
tout peut s'oublier
qui s'en fui déjà
oublier les temps de malentendus
et le temps perdu
à savoir comment
oublier ces heures
qui tuaient parfaois
à coups de pourquoi
le coeur de bonheur
ne me quitte pas ...

x: and i lean into you. my mouth close to your ear. i whisper softly, "i wonder if she knows brel wasn't french at all. brel was actually belgian."

danny: i can't understand what she's singing.

x: i'll translate:

"it is necessary to forget.
everything that has already flown
can be forgotten.
the times

filled with misunderstandings
the times lost
trying to understand
how to forget those hours
that kill the heart of happiness
with just a simple "'why?'"

danny: what does *"ne me quitte pas"* mean?

x: don't leave me.

danny: don't leave me.

x: you will wake up at 3am. you will think you hear footsteps in your living room. you will think there is someone in your apartment. but you are completely alone.

danny: don't leave me.

x: you are completely and totally alone. and you will toss and turn. you will reach out for a stack of blank postcards from our trip to paris you've started keeping by your bed. you will look at them and for some reason you will remember. the flight. the hotel. the sites. as much as you don't want to, you will remember.

danny: don't leave me.

x: you will remember paris. you will remember *"ne me quitte pas."* you will remember you are in new york city. it is october, 2001.

2.

(danny wakes up. he is alone, in his bed. he reaches for a phone and dials.)

danny: hey, it's me … pick up. i can't sleep.

(the lights go out.)

3.

(danny is at the cock, a bar in the east village. the atmosphere is trendy/trashy. on the bar, a go-go boy dances, wearing only a pair of boxer briefs and a pair of boots. beatrice sits at the other end of the bar, drinking wine and wearing a red dress. danny is scoping the room, his back to the bar. the go-go boy squats down on the bar behind danny.)

go-go boy: *(to danny.)* i see a very hungry puppy.

danny: *(handing over a dollar without even looking at him.)* do you want me to tell you you're hot?

go-go boy: i should be paying you.

(danny raises his head. he coolly assesses the go-go boy.)

go-go boy: you getting any action?

danny: the guys here bore me.

go-go boy: they're all looking at you.

danny: only because you're standing next to me in your underwear.

go-go boy: so … am i boring you?

danny: i don't know yet.

go-go boy: you're cocky.

danny: yeah, that's me.

(the go-go boy reaches over and kisses danny.)

go-go boy: i'm very, very hard. i want you to pull me out right here in front of everyone. stroke me while you drink your beer.

danny: *that* would be cocky, wouldn't it?

go-go boy: would you do it? would you dare?

danny: only if you keep your shorts on. i like them.

(the go-go boy takes danny's hand into his shorts.)

go-go boy: ever fuck on an airplane?

danny: no.

go-go boy: i think fucking on an airplane is hot, don't you?

(danny notices beatrice.)

danny: there's a woman at the bar.

go-go boy: don't worry about her. she performs here.

danny: she's staring at us.

go-go boy: *(as if it explained the whole thing)* she's french.

danny: she freaks me out.

go-go boy: she's about to go on. she'll leave us alone.

danny: is she any good?

go-go boy: define good.

(beatrice gets up from the bar and goes over to the stage. the room reverberates with the sound of her heels clicking on the floor. on the way, she and danny look at each other. the moment is tense. she walks past him and steps onstage. she addresses the audience.)

beatrice: *messieurs, je m'appelle beatrice* and i wish you a *bon soir. bon soir? oui, bon soir.* those words do not sit well with me tonight, *messieurs. non.* it is not a *bon soir.* this place. the smoke. go-go *garçon* over there. and all of you … so many of you … and yet, so much loneliness. how many of you, *messieurs,* will take someone home, so you do not end up like those unlucky *messieur*s who don't. those unfortunate ones who lie completely and totally alone, staring out their window all night until the sun rises. the ones who lay in bed, sleepless and petrified. *bon soir?* no, not for them. they lie still, listening to every creek on their floorboards, wondering if someone has come into their apartment to assault them. and wouldn't that be preferable to that insufferable loneliness, *messieurs*? to be invaded – it is a scary thing, or perhaps very beautiful … sometimes i cannot tell the difference. *(she looks around.)* you don't understand a damn thing i'm saying, do you? *(sighs)* *d'accord.* what do i care? i don't care at all. it reminds me of a song. a song about someone who cared too much and after listening to this, you still won't care. and i still won't care. and that is preferable, i suppose … to … to … wanting. and for that … *(she looks at danny.)* i dedicate this to you.

(she begins to sing "ne me quitte pas." danny mouths the words. the go-go boy leans into him and whispers in his ear:)

go-go boy: you speak french?

danny: excuse me?

go-go boy: you know the words.

danny: i gotta go to the bathroom for a minute. i don't feel well.

(he runs to the bathroom.)

4.

(danny locks himself into the bathroom stall. there is a sudden silence. it is as if everyone has disappeared from the world and danny is left, alone. he pulls out his cellphone.)

danny: hey, pick up. this is getting humiliating. why don't you call me? i can't sleep anymore. i keep hearing people in my apartment and –

(suddenly there is a knocking at the bathroom stall.)

beatrice: *monsieur?*

(danny opens the door to the stall. beatrice stands there with two glasses.)

danny: what do you want?

beatrice: go-go *garçon* said you were not feeling well. i thought you had had too much to drink, so i brought you something fizzy to settle your stomach.

danny: champagne?

beatrice: i am french, what do i know? if you are throwing up, you might as well have champagne, *non?*

(she extends the drink.)

danny: *(taking the drink.)* thanks, but there's nothing wrong with my stomach.

beatrice: so much the better.

(she extends her hand.)

beatrice: i am beatrice.

danny: i know.

beatrice: do you have a name, *mon beau garçon?*

danny: danny.

beatrice: *enchante*, danny.

(she raises her glass.)

beatrice: to jacques brel.

danny: who?

beatrice: jacques brel. the man who wrote the song i was singing. the one i dedicated to you.

danny: you didn't really.

beatrice: you knew the words.

danny: isn't that like a famous french song?

beatrice: brel was belgian. did you know that? i'm sure you did. it is unusual i run into someone who knows brel. none of those ... those *imbeciles* outside know anything about him or anything worthwhile.

danny: i'm sure some of them do. it's no big deal.

beatrice: of course it is! the world is overrun by mediocrity and the american homosexuals are not immune. but, you ... you are far from mediocre. you are exceptional. you made go-go *garçon* look hideous. and for that i bought you champagne. go-go *garçon* is too conceited.

(she raises her glass again.)

beatrice: so, to jacques brel?

danny: *(raising his glass.)* whatever you say.

(they drink.)

beatrice: may i come in?

danny: what for?

beatrice: there is something i need to discuss with you.

(she comes in and closes the door behind her.)

beatrice: it is something about you ... your face ... your eyes ... you are, how do they say, exotic?

danny: my parents. they're cuban.

beatrice: ah, yes ... it is very fashionable to be *exotic* these days, eh?. i should know. but ... that is not it. there are many many boys who are *exotic.* many many boys who offer exactly what you do. and yet ... you are incredibly desirable.

danny: i do alright.

beatrice: you do more than alright. i think you are a ... how do americans say it? a heartbreaker?

danny: is that what you think?

beatrice: perhaps not. a heartbreaker would not know brel. a heartbreaker would not understand "ne me quitte pas." *"laisse-moi devenir l'ombre de ton ombre, l'ombre de ta main, l'ombre de ton chien."* you are the one who has his heart broken. that is what makes you special.

danny: i think you were right the first time.

beatrice: *ne me trompes pas.* i have no time for that, *mon beau* danny. i have been looking for someone with the heart that trips all over itself because it is broken.

(she presses her hand against his chest.)

beatrice: you cannot lie to me now. i can feel it. it is the same. look.

(she takes his hand and puts it to her chest.)

beatrice: don't you see?

danny: it's beating so fast.

beatrice: as is yours, *mon chère.* see, you are special. and i have wanted a special person to share something very special with.

danny: what?

(she points to something scribbled on the wall.)

danny: *(reading.)* "abandon every hope, all you who enter."

beatrice: i came in here one night and read that and i thought to myself, "*mon dieu!* the voice of reason!"

danny: "abandon every hope, all you who enter."

beatrice: you understand these words! you feel them. do you know how many people make the piss and shit and snort god-knows-what in this toilette and do not read ... do not comprehend these words? i ask myself who wrote them? where did they come from? i think you know.

danny: no, i don't. i don't know anything. excuse me.

(he turns to go.)

beatrice: who were you calling on the phone?

danny: no one.

beatrice: "why don't you call me?" who is this man who makes someone like you even ask this?

danny: you heard wrong. look, thanks for the champagne, but buying me a drink doesn't give you the right to ... to eavesdrop. it's none of your business.

beatrice: that is not so. i can prove it.

danny: fine. prove it.

beatrice: we are both not american.

danny: i am american.

beatrice: even though you say you are cuban?

danny: my parents are cuban. i am not cuban.

beatrice: yes, but you look cuban. you have the exotic look. it is undeniable. you must know what it is like to feel ... different. you must know what it is like to not be able to claim this soil as your soil.

danny: i don't think most people out there can claim new york as their soil. it's no big deal. it doesn't make me special. it doesn't make you special. people move. it's normal.

beatrice: i did not move. i was forced to leave my country.

danny: *why?*

beatrice: paris is a cemetery. all the buildings are made of tombstones. oh, yes, the rest of the world thinks it is very beautiful –

danny: –it is.

beatrice: ah, so you have been? you have strolled *les champs-elysees.* sat in *le café flore.* visited *notre-dame.* and you find it all romantic. *le vin rouge? les galouises? l'histoire?* but you are really, very stupid, *mon beau garçon.* do not take it personally. there is something a tourist does not understand. a parisian. a real parisian has a special skill. we know *la mort.* we can see ghosts. they are all around us, because we are all concerned with the past. with our memories, our monuments. paris is an embalmed corpse. but even the embalming cannot stop the rot, the smell, the decay. and we are reminded that soon we all too will decay like that. it is fate. lately, it had gotten unbearable. unknown to most foreigners, a secret fad began to spread around paris. it became tout la mode to devise more and more unusual ways of committing suicide. i had to escape. i wanted life. i ended up in new york.

i practiced my english. i tried to blend in. and then came *le jour tragique en semptembre,* i realized that i will never be an american. *la mort* had come to new york and all the new yorkers were angry, sad, upset ... and i ... i was resigned. i never felt more parisian in my life. it broke my heart, *mon beau garçon.* it is the same as you. it is the same as "why don't you call me?"

danny: no it isn't.

beatrice: *(muttered to herself.)* abandon every hope, all you who enter.

(she pulls out some pills and takes some with her champagne.)

danny: what are you doing?

beatrice: death by anti-depressants. it's very esoteric.

danny: what kind of anti-depressants?

beatrice: they are called madeleines. would you like some?

danny: will these kill me?

beatrice: very, very, very slowly.

(he takes a couple and swallows them.)

beatrice: you will feel better in a little while. now, i have to get out there for my next song. come out and see me sing, please … i will also dedicate it to you.

(she exits. the scene changes. it is vague. we see beatrice on stage in front of the microphone. "ne me quitte pas" begins again. like in the previous dream, her manner is abstracted so she recedes into the background of the scene.)

beatrice: *moi je t'offrirai*
des perles de pluie
venues de pays
où il ne pleut pas
je creuserai la terre
jusqu'aprés ma mort
pour couvrir ton corps
d'or et de lumière
je f'rai un domaine
où l'amour sera roi
où l'amour sera loi
où tu seras reine
ne me quitte pas …

(x appears.)

5.

x: you are dreaming, danny boy.

danny: tell me what she's singing.

x: *i will offer you*
pearls of rain
brought from a land
where it never rains.
i will cross the earth
even after my death
to cover your body
with gold and light.
i will make a kingdom
where love will be king
where love will be law ...

danny: what does *"ne me quitte pas"* mean again?

x: don't leave me.

danny: no, it doesn't.

(danny gets up and begins to run.)

x: you wonder what is going on. you wonder if you have fallen asleep and woken up in some other city. this does not feel like your city. your city does not smell of burning. your city is not plastered with flyers of missing persons. with flowers and candles. you find yourself in the union square subway station and you stop and look at the faces covering the walls. you have to. and what are you expecting to see? the face of someone you recognize? instead, your eye catches a picture of a woman wearing a red dress.

(the picture speaks to danny. it is beatrice. she speaks with an american accent.)

beatrice: my name is beatrice. i do not smile. i stare at you cold. hard. you avert your gaze. you want another face. another name. so you look at the next flyer. the same red dress. next flyer. the same face. next flyer. no smile. next flyer. same stare. the same words repeated over and over again – "last seen," "please call," "any information appreciated." my name is beatrice. i worked on the 90th floor. and you know you should not have looked. you know you should not have noticed my name. you know you should not allow your mind to flirt with specifics. not now. you decide to catch your train home and then you hear it.

("ne me quitte pas" reverberates throughout the station.)

beatrice: you run. you need to get out of the train station. you go outside. you want to run away. far. away from the fliers and through the streets. you are scared. the air smells like ashes. your hand reaches into your pocket and pulls out your cell phone. you hand is about to dial his number, when you notice you have a message.

x: *(on the phone.)* i'm sorry i haven't called you earlier. i'm in paris. i can't remember even buying the ticket or what i'm doing here, but … well, i want to say everything reminds me of … i don't know … but, it's different. completely different. i wish i could come home, but i can't. i hope you are understanding me, danny boy.

danny: i am dreaming. i am dreaming. i am dreaming.

(darkness.)

6.

(we are on an airplane. danny is asleep in one seat. magda is sitting next to him. they are bathed in the glow of the overhead reading lights. danny wakes up.)

danny: where am i?

magda: somewhere over the ocean. we took off a couple hours ago.

danny: *(noticing magda.)* where did you come from?

magda: *(pointing.)* a seat back there. how are you able to sleep? did you take a sleeping pill?

danny: i always do these days.

magda: *no es mala idea.* i am so nervous, but isn't everyone nervous when they fly these days? i am completely petrified. how i got on board, i don't know. all the security did nothing to calm me down. don't those pills … you know … *disorientate* you? i tried to get my doctor to give me something before i came. but he said no. you get addicted. my mother offered to talk to her doctor – a nice, cuban doctor who will write you a prescription for anything you want because his father used to know her father in matanzas.

danny: *(aside.)* i can't be sitting next to a cuban. *(to magda.)* you weren't here when we took off.

magda: i saw you traveling alone and you were asleep and you looked so … *(it's like she knows the word, but decides not to say it.)* … i wanted to sit next to you. i switched my seat when you were asleep. you remind me of my son. *(she offers her hand.)* i'm magda.

danny: danny.

magda: just danny or *(spanish pronunciation.)* daniel?

danny: danny works better than *(exaggerated "gringo" pronunciation.)* "daniehlle."

magda: you shouldn't change your name … even if others mispronounce it. that's not your fault. no one changes their name when this thick accent of mine ruins it.

danny: there's nothing wrong with your accent.

magda: i am an immigrant or in exile as most people in miami say. have you ever been to miami?

danny: that's where i'm from.

magda: really?

danny: don't tell anyone.

magda: our secret.

danny: did you connect in new york?

magda: what … ? oh, yes. you know, it was much cheaper than going direct. but, flying into new york –

danny: –just a small layover and then you're off to paris.

magda: when they said that to me –

danny: –don't say it.

magda: when they told me i had to go to new york … *(she offers up her arm. her hand is shaking.)* look at how i got. just to think–

danny: –don't think about that.

magda: let me tell you something. i am a nurse and in my kind of work. you wake up every morning thinking you might have to deal with *la muerte.* you would think because it's part of my job that i would be used to it … but she comes and i am always … *sorprendida.*

danny: why are you going to paris?

magda: i'm hoping to spend some time with my son. he … lives there now. and you?

danny: i don't know. maybe it was the cheap airfare.

magda: the cheap airfare. *(silence.)* first time?

danny: no. i was there five-six months ago. it was springtime. it was warm and the men and the women are just like in the movies. they're really beautiful and they sit in these outdoor cafes, smoking and drinking and you want to smoke and drink too because if they could do it and look good … but you end up feeling like such an american. *(he looks outside the window.)* it's probably really cold there now.

magda: my son tells me the same things about the cafes in his postcards.

danny: he sends you postcards?

magda: yes. i brought them with me so i can visit all the places he tells me about.

danny: i like postcards. they prove you were some place.

magda: i'm worried about speaking french. do you speak french?

danny: very, very little.

magda: it can't be too hard if you already speak spanish.

danny: i don't speak spanish anymore. i forgot.

magda: *por que?*

danny: just because.

(magda leans over danny and looks out the window with him.)

magda: it's so quiet out there. it makes you think you're safe. isn't that funny?

danny: yeah, it's really funny.

(magda reaches out and smooths danny's hair.)

magda: *duermete, hijo.*

danny: please don't touch me.

(she removes her hand. the lights go out.)

7.

(magda alone. she reads from a postcard.)

magda: i found this stack of postcards
we meant to address and send
to all our friends
telling them what a wonderful time
we had in paris.
cheesy pictures
of the eiffel tower,
the pyramid at the *louvre*,
the cafés in st. germain.
we meant to send them
but they ended up blank and empty
i suppose this is because we had such a good time.
i'm using them now.
i'm sending you as many
"wish you were here"s
as i can.
love ...

(the lights go out.)

8.

(we are in paris. danny is standing in the lobby of his hotel in the marais. a concierge stands behind the front desk.)

danny: *excusez moi ... je ne parlais français. parlez vous anglais, sil vous plait?*

concierge: you must be ... how do you say? *le jetlag?*

danny: yes, *le jetlag.*

concierge: that explains it. for a minute i was insulted you would think me some sadistic parisian. does your memory fail you or cannot you remember that i speak the english?

danny: remember?

concierge: *oui, monsieur.* i was here last spring when you visited with your handsome friend. is he with you?

danny: it's just me.

concierge: well, you are staying in *le marais.* you should have no problem making friends here, *oui?*

danny: i'm sorry i forgot. i just … didn't want to be rude. i didn't want to assume you spoke english. you hear all these stories about the french. i mean …

concierge: *monsieur,* let me tell you a secret. in *l'ecole,* the teacher will humiliate you if you do not speak perfectly. so we are afraid of english unless we speak it without error. and for most of us, that is impossible, so we will not speak it because we do not want to be thought of as stupid.

danny: well, i'm the stupid one.

concierge: *non!* you are *en vancances!* you will not be stupid in paris. if there is anyone who will be stupid, it will be me. *(he smiles.)* welcome back.

danny: is my room ready?

concierge: it is the room just by the stairs on the second floor, overlooking the street.

danny: is that the room i stayed in before?

concierge: *oui, monsieur,* you were most explicit in your e-mail.

danny: good.

concierge: *monsieur,* it is not my way to intrude … but, i must offer an alternative, which may appeal to you. we have many vacancies as the recent events have made it difficult for people to travel … i can put you in another room where you may be more comfortable? a suite! top floor! i can give it to you for the same price.

danny: *(taking a deep breath.)* no. i want my room.

concierge: perhaps you are here to bring up memories, but what are memories? what are ghosts to an american? nothing! they should not concern you ... so young ... able to travel. to escape. to change. if you want my advice, i would enjoy this new vacances and try to forget. to start with, i can make some dinner recommendations ...

danny: yes, i liked that place in the *place des vosges* last time. can you make a reservation?

concierge: i am sorry. i cannot recommend it. how about this little place on *rue de vielle de temple?* very good *confit de carnard.* oh! and you must try their *tarte tartin!* yes! i will ring them up at this instant. and after dinner, there is le amnesia café across the street. i am sure there will be something there that will please monsieur.

danny: i will eat at the *place des vosges.* thank you.

concierge: very well ... but you must go to amnesia café. you will be very popular there, i'm sure.

danny: does amnesia café pay you or something?

concierge: *monsieur,* i am paid to know what a tourist wants even before he knows it himself!

danny: and amnesia café is what i want?

concierge: i guarantee it!

danny: we'll see about that.

concierge: *(holding up the key.)* promise me i will see you come back later quite drunk and *trés jolie* or it is the top floor suite for you!

danny: fine.

concierge: very good.

danny: *(grabbing the key.)* *merci beaucoup.*

concierge: *de rien, monsieur.*

(danny runs to his room. magda enters with her bags, reading a postcard.)

magda: i am thinking of the hotel
we stayed in
in the *marais.*
i am thinking of the
four poster bed,
the tiny bottles of red wine in the fridge,
the bathtub with a handheld shower,
and the window i would open
to look down onto the street
at the parisian men
with their cigarettes dangling from their mouths.
i stared at them the way you stare at the scenery.
which made me want
to reach out for you
and pull you on the bed.
i think about your body
on that bed.
i think about how
beautiful
the city made you.
love …

(she approaches the front desk.)

concierge: *madame?*

magda: i would like a room, *sil vous plait.*

(darkness.)

9.

(we are in amnesia café, a gay bar in the marais. kenny sits at the bar. he does not drink. danny sits next to him. they are staring intently at a bartender, who has his back to them. the bartender is staring into a mirror that hangs over the length of the bar, muttering to himself, smoking.)

danny: *(staring over at kenny.)* how long has he been doing that?

kenny: i have n-n-no idea.

danny: i want a drink. should we gang up on him? he must have smoked a whole pack of marlboros by now.

kenny: you'd think they would smoke g-g-gal *(he gives up.)* you know, those famous french cigarettes.

danny: *(offering his pack.)* galouises? they're the blonde ones.

kenny: can i?

(kenny takes a cigarette. danny offers to light it.)

kenny: oh, i don' smoke. *(beat. he holds the cigarette, unlit, like a prop.)* do i look really american?

danny: you're not drinking. i figured you were as clueless as i was.

kenny: i am afraid of the b-b-b-b-bartender. i don't do too well ordering drinks at home, much less here in french.

danny: i'm danny.

kenny: kenny. where are you from?

danny: new york.

kenny: me too. you're pretty cute for a *touriste americain.*

danny: high school french won't get you far, *mon ami. (he looks over at the bartender).* god damn him. what do you suppose he's doing?

kenny: he's been muttering all night. i wish i could figure out what he's saying.

(the bartender becomes audible. somehow only he and danny are privy to the words.)

bartender: you called me.
you told me you were going to new york.
last minute.
unexpected.
and i wondered
was there something
about my face?
my looks?
my body
prone before you?
"pin me down," i begged.
"pin me down."
the cold wind in paris
is very old,
a messenger from the catacombs.
pin me down and
warm me, please.
i went to the cafes,
i went to the bars,
i went to the restaurants
you go to
hoping you were there.
hoping you were really a coward
and had lied to me.
i would rather your betrayal
than disappearance from paris
and reappearance in new york
where you are dead to me.

(the scene resumes.)

kenny: what did he say?

danny: *(lies.)* i have no idea.

kenny: you looked like you understood.

danny: no, i didn't.

(the bartender turns to them.)

bartender: are you making fun of me?

danny: what's so important you couldn't get us some drinks?

bartender: i was struck by inspiration. i was composing a song. a very sad song about heartbreak.

danny: you're like that guy ... what's his name? jacques brel?

bartender: jacques brel is shit. he was really belgian.

danny: we all have to come from somewhere.

bartender: but the belgians are hopeless.

danny: what do you have against belgians?

bartender: one of those sons of bitches broke my heart.

(he leaves.)

kenny: well, you're worse at ordering drinks than me.

danny: is it me, or is he like really ugly?

kenny: are you kidding? his eyes ... *(he looks at danny.)* your eyes look just like that.

danny: do they? then i must be very ugly.

kenny: incredibly. i want to kiss you.

danny: no you don't.

kenny: do you think i sound retarded?

danny: vulnerable.

kenny: i'm not. j-j-just nervous. i can't speak the language.

danny: i'm sorry. i meant … i didn't really notice.

(he turns towards the window looking out on the street. he notices magda staring into the bar. she sees him. she runs off.)

danny: ever wonder why they call this place amnesia café?

kenny: i never thought about it.

danny: what are you supposed to forget in here?

kenny: i don't know. what are you trying to forget?

danny: nothing.

(he reaches over and kisses kenny. the action is pretty frantic. desperate.)

danny: you're shaking.

kenny: so are you.

(danny wraps his arms around kenny. he pulls kenny's head to his chest. the music suddenly drops. the silence is vast, like the eye of a gay bar hurricane.)

kenny: i can hear your heart beat.

danny: really?

kenny: i can hear your pulse. in your neck. in your wrist. i can hear your eyelashes. i think that's really beautiful.

danny: you're so warm …

kenny: are you alone in paris?

danny: completely.

(darkness.)

10.

(a light comes on. we are in a hotel room. madga holding a postcard.)

magda: what was the thing about the men here?
they look at you.
they stare.
they're shameless.
we'd see which one of us they liked more.
and even though you spoke the language
and read the maps
and ordered the food,
i won that game every time.

(the light goes out.)

11.

(the light comes on. x is in bed with a tourist guide to paris. the door opens. danny comes in. he is in shorts, t-shirt and running shoes.)

danny: are you still in bed?

x: i'm feeling very, very lazy.

danny: well, i'm feeling very, very hungry. i want one of those *café crèmes* and a whole basket of croissants. i don't care about the carbs.

x: you don't need to care about the carbs.

danny: it takes a lot of caring to keep me up, okay?

(danny jumps in bed.)

x: oh, man, you are stinky.

danny: you like it.

x: is that why you do it? humiliate yourself jogging all over paris to get musky?

danny: i got checked out.

x: they were wondering who let out the crazy american.

danny: *(putting his head on x's chest.)* you're just jealous.

x: yeah, why can't i be as american as you?

danny: what are you reading?

x: this thing on georges-eugene haussman

danny: who was he?

x: he was supposed to modernize paris so you could find something like the *arc de triomphe* and find your way home, wherever that is.

danny: that is total bullshit.

x: no it's not. paris makes sense. it's impossible to get lost here.

danny: i got lost. i began to jog, trying to remember the way back. trying to keep in mind where the seine was so i could figure out direction … but i got turned around.

x: did you ask for directions?

danny: i asked someone "marais?" and they pointed.

x: *(pulling off danny's shirt.)* and they didn't kidnap you standing there all sweaty and musky?

danny: oh, yeah, kidnap the stupid, smelly american.

x: *(putting his hand inside danny's shorts.)* you're not stupid, danny boy. not stupid at all.

danny: but i'm smelly right?

(they kiss and lay down on the bed. darkness.)

12.

(magda reading a postcard.)

magda: i was never able to make out the maps,
could not determine direction.
even now,
standing in the middle of manhattan,
i stare uptown.
i stare downtown.
even here,
at home,
i cannot discern the landscape.
everything has changed,
the skyline dissolving.
the city has become foreign.
love ...

13.

(danny turns on a light. kenny is now in bed next to him.)

kenny: *(waking up.)* what's wrong?

danny: i heard something. i thought someone was in the room with us.

kenny: you were dreaming, danny boy.

danny: don't call me that.

kenny: isn't that your name?

danny: my name is *(spanish pronunciation.) daniel.* it's just that most people can only manage "danny."

kenny: *daniel.* i like it. it's–

kenny: –if you say exotic, i may have to kill you.

kenny: i was going to say it sounds important. much more so than just "danny." danny boy.

danny: *daniel.*

kenny: let's go back to sleep, *daniel.*

danny: i have a bunch of cigarette filters stuck in my throat. i need water ... want some?

kenny: not french hotel water.

danny: *(taking a sip.)* it tastes like evian.

(he holds out the bottle.)

kenny: how do i know this isn't spiked?

danny: you saw me open the bottle. you saw me take a sip. don't you trust me?

kenny: you're giving me your cooties.

danny: you can't say cooties in paris. it's against the law to be that american.

(kenny takes the water.)

kenny: after what we did, why should cooties matter?

danny: after what we *did?*

kenny: you fucked me.

danny: you didn't like it?

kenny: you were on top of me. and you were looking at me. and there was a look on your face … it was b-b-beautiful … and you were pushing into me. and you asked if you could … you didn't have a c-c-condom on and you asked if you could … and you were looking at me like there's no one you wanted more than me … and you asked if you could and i said yes.

danny: it's no big deal.

kenny: so you do it a lot?

danny: you got to go home with me. i sucked your cock. i fucked you. i'm spent. disposable. done. over. you'll walk out of here tomorrow and by the time you're done with your coffee, i won't exist. so, don't worry about my cooties.

kenny: do you want me to forget about you?

danny: why aren't you stuttering?

kenny: i don't *really* stutter. i tremble. i woke up a few months ago and i couldn't stop shaking. my hands. my jaw. it's hard to keep it under control. my muscles hurt. my spine got tired of trying to stay rigid, so it gave out on me. a friend of mine recommended a homeopathic ch-ch-chiropractor. the chiropractor told me to get off caffeine, sugar, alcohol. and sure enough, the shaking stopped. i. could speak perfectly and my spine relaxed and became long again. my chiropractor said i made progress, but i missed coffee. i missed chocolate. so i came to paris–

danny: –and i'm your sugar fix?

kenny: try living in fear of sweets.

danny: i'm way ahead of you. there's a big gooey *crêpe* just calling out to me and i'm trying not to listen. last time i was here–

kenny: –when was that?

danny: last spring.

kenny: where did you have *crêpes?*

danny: near *notre-dame.* there's a *crêpe* stand there. i ordered in my best french *"un crêpe du banana et nutella, sil vous plait"*. the nutella just melts and gets all gooey and your lips end up covered with it and my … my … ex boyfriend kissed me in front of *notre-dame.* and kissing him there i couldn't help thinking how this shit couldn't be good for me, no matter how good it tasted … we stayed in this hotel. in this room. he fucked me on this bed.

kenny: *(weirded out.)* really?

danny: i wanted to stay here. sleep here. remember him on top of me. looking at me with that look on his face … it was beautiful … and i exploded. i totally exploded. i … i guess i was in love and i guessed he was too. he told me. he said, "i love you." i remember that. his face. his mouth making the words. i love you. but …

kenny: were you trying to get me to say i love you?

danny: no, that would be stupid.

kenny: well, so are chocolates. so are cigarettes. so is alcohol. i love you.

danny: we just met. you don't love me. right now, nobody loves me.

kenny: i don't care. i want to be foolish. i want to be out of my mind. say it. i love you.

danny: i'd be lying. you're lying.

kenny: you're in paris. you have to say it. just say it once, please. if you say it enough, you believe it.

danny: i … i love you.

kenny: louder.

danny: i love you.

kenny: again.

danny: i love you.

kenny: i love you too

danny: *(breaking down.)* i love you i love you i love you i love you

kenny: just keep saying it. it will feel better, i promise.

(darkness.)

14.

(the light comes on again. we are in magda's room. she reads from another postcard.)

magda: the sun will be rising soon
and i am still awake
trying to remember the *marais*
as the streets are waking up.
the street washers leaving a trail of shiny cobblestones,
the *patisseries* and *boulengeries* laying out their window displays,
and here i am
scared
with nothing to look forward to.
not a *croissant,*

not a *tartine*,
not even a cup of coffee.

(darkness.)

15.

(danny turns on a light. x is in bed next to him.)

x: what's wrong?

danny: i thought i heard someone in the room with us.

x: you were dreaming, danny boy.

danny: no i wasn't.

x: go back to sleep.

danny: tell me what we should do tomorrow.

x: why?

danny: because you know everything. you have it planned out. i know you do.

x: i thought either the *louvre* or *pere-lachaise.*

danny: what's *pere-lachaise?*

x: it's a famous cemetery.

danny: it's a little too night of the living dead for me.

x: if you don't want to go, we don't have to go. i thought it would be fun.

danny: but you want to go. you had it planned. you probably wouldn't have told me until we got on the metro.

x: well, i can go by myself and meet you somewhere. that way you can do something you want to do.

danny: like what?

x: what do you want to do?

danny: it doesn't matter. i'm going to get lost. i'm not going to be able to speak the language and i'm not going to be able to meet you anywhere.

x: stay in the marais. or just take a cab. the cab driver will know where to go. we can meet somewhere easy, like the pyramid at the *louvre*.

danny: i don't want to be alone.

x: you were fine yesterday ...

danny: i want to do something together.

x: okay, fine. we'll do something together.

danny: i love you.

x: i love you too, danny boy.

danny: say it again.

x: sleep.

(darkness.)

16.

(danny wakes up. it is morning. he is alone.)

danny: kenny?

(he gets out of bed and opens the curtains, letting the light in. he throws on a shirt and pants and puts on his shoes. his cell phone rings. he picks it up.)

danny: hello?

(no answer. he picks up the hotel phone and dials the concierge.)

concierge: *bon jour, monsieur.*

danny: did you call my cell phone?

concierge: why would i do that, *monsieur?*

danny: someone called my phone and it was a paris number.

concierge: curious, *monsieur*, but i would have used the hotel's phone.

danny: i suppose.

concierge: what is on the agenda today?

danny: you tell me.

concierge: *notre-dame.* today i am feeling *notre-dame.*

danny: fine. *merci.*

concierge: *de rien, monsieur.*

(danny runs out.)

17.

(danny is on the street. kenny appears eating a pastry.)

danny: getting your sugar rush?

kenny: i'm sorry? do i know you?

danny: amnesia café?

kenny: i have no idea what you're talking about.

danny: *hôtel de la bretonnerie?*

kenny: i'm staying at the *caron de beaumarchais.*

danny: you slept at the *bretonnerie* last night.

kenny: i think you've mistaken me for someone else. excuse me.

(kenny runs off. danny's cell phone rings.)

danny: hello?

(x is on the phone.)

x: i know why you're in paris.

danny: did you call me earlier? where are you?

x: who else would call you here? i figured …

danny: you figured i'd follow you.

x: i wanted you to come. i'm worried, danny boy. i want to see you. find me, please.

danny: where are you? where should i go?

x: *l'inferno.* it's a bar.

danny: where is it.?

x: *l'inferno.* find it. i'll be waiting.

(he hangs up. danny collapses. darkness.)

18.

(danny is dreaming. beatrice, very chic, very tragic, very edith piaf stands in front of a microphone. danny watches her from the floor.)

beatrice: the people ask me if i miss paris. if i miss strolling down *les champs d'elysees.* smoking a cigarette. a sexy *gamine* ala leslie caron looking for her gene kelly. if i miss *les café crèmes.* the r's roaring in the back of my throat, growling like an angry bitch on a leash. and i wonder if something is wrong with me? i never remember those things.

i have never even seen the film *an american in paris.*

someone should make *a parisienne in new york.* i will see that. i want to know what happens to her. i want to see the close up on her face when she realizes what happens when something escapes your life. it vanishes. and she thought paris was the city of ghosts. the city of *la mort.* but, she misunderstood what *la mort* was. the woman she was, she does not remember. not the drinks in an anonymous bar. nor the american songs she'd sing in french. nor the men ... the countless men she'd kiss on their necks to taste their sweat or drink their pulse. that woman has vanished. and when something vanishes like that, it is dead. i want to see the close up on her face when she realizes she has died and no one bothered to tell her.

now if you excuse me, i don't think i'll sing the next song. i have to change my dress for the second act.

(darkness. end of part one.)

part two

1.

(danny and x.)

x: you should try to pick up some phrases before we go.

danny: why? you speak french enough for the two of us.

x: what if you get lost? how will you find your way? besides, they're horrible to americans if you don't make some effort.

danny: i suck at languages.

x: you speak spanish. it shouldn't be that hard.

danny: i forgot all my spanish.

x: don't be difficult.

danny: fine. you want to teach me french? go ahead. give me a useful phrase.

x: *vous rêvez.*

danny: what does that mean?

x: you are dreaming.

danny: and that's useful how?

x: *ne me quitte pas.*

danny: what does that mean?

x: don't leave me.

danny: are you sure these will be useful?

x: one more and you'll know all you need. *où est l'inferno?*

danny: where is the inferno?

x: that's it. now you can speak french.

(darkness.)

2.

(danny is at the concierge desk.)

concierge: *monsieur*, are you alright? have you come to your senses?

danny: i'm fine. i was just dizzy outside.

concierge: you are most fortunate, i just happened to look outside and there you were passed out on the street. i thought you had jumped from your room.

danny: i'm on the second floor.

concierge: you could have jumped very hard.

danny: well, i'm fine. i was hungover.

concierge: ah, yes! i saw you last night coming in *très jolie* with *un beau garçon!*

danny: you saw us?

concierge: with my own eyes.

danny: i must be on crack.

concierge: if you want my opinion, monsieur, it is *le fatiguè*. it is coming early this year.

danny: *le fatiguè?*

concierge: the pollution, it is terrible in paris. it gets worse when it gets colder, pressing down on you. it is so you cannot stand on *le métro* or even walk for a few minutes to the *marché*. the *pharmacie* on *rue de rivoli* has excellent pills for *le fatiguè*. would you like me to ring them?

danny: no that's alright. listen, do you know if there's a way to trace a call? someone … a friend called me on this phone. they are in paris, but i don't know where. i have called the number back and there is no ring tone.

concierge: we must put our faith in people, not machines. i do not like those little phones. there are certain things not meant to go in the pocket, *monsieur*.

danny: american convenience.

concierge: you are *en vacances!* no need for convenience here! you are in paris!

danny: i am looking for a bar or a café named *l'inferno*.

concierge: why do you want to go there?

danny: someone told me about it.

concierge: and who was that?

danny: a friend.

concierge: i have not heard of it.

danny: ah, well … thanks. if you hear of it, please let me know. i'm supposed to meet my friend there.

concierge: *d'accord.* do you know, monsieur, that in dante, the center of the inferno is very, very cold and made of ice?

danny: that's a book, right?

concierge: it is a poem, *monsieur*.

danny: is there a bookstore around?

concierge: *les bon mots* down the street. would you like me to call and see if there is a copy of the *inferno?* i cannot guarantee it, but they have racy magazines that might interest monsieur.

danny: would they have a copy in english?

concierge: i do not know. but i'm sure you will do fine with the french.

danny: why do you say that?

concierge: you have been practicing, monsieur.

danny: i have?

concierge: *(unaccented.) monsieur,* we are speaking french right now.

danny: what did you say?

concierge: *(back to the accent.) monsieur*, you are disoriented.

danny: i don't speak french.

concierge: don't be humble with me. go get your book and sit down with a *café crème.* i'm sure you will be fine … and then you can stroll down to *notre-dame.*

danny: oh, yes, you were feeling *notre-dame.*

concierge: the light through the stained glass should be exquisite today.

(darkness.)

3.

(danny turns on his cell phone.)

danny: hey, it's me. you have to call me back. i have no idea where this inferno is. you need to tell me the *arrondisment*. the metro stop. something. call me back. i'll keep the phone on.

4.

(danny is at les bon mots, the gay bookstore in the marais. an attendant gives him the eye.)

attendant: i see you.

danny: pardon?

attendant: don't think you can walk in here with those jeans and not be noticed by me. i notice all. turn around. yes. they fit you quite well, both in front and back.

danny: i was wondering if you could help me.

attendant: in every way i can. do you live around here?

danny: i'm visiting from new york.

attendant: american?

danny: do you like americans?

attendant: *(winking.)* i have my fantasies. now, i would very much like to see you walk around this store in your levis.

danny: they're from the gap.

attendant: you are trying to seduce me, you crazy american! you with your perfect ass and your perfect french.

danny: that good, huh?

attendant: do you know how difficult it is for an american to speak french so well? it is impossible! you aren't tortured in *l'ecole* like the french. one teacher used to strike me with a ruler across the bottom if i did not properly learn the subjunctive tense. it is no accident the marquis de sade was french, *cheri.* so, command me. i live to serve you.

danny: i need a copy of a book. dante's *inferno.*

attendant: such a smart book. you must have a very, very big brain. is the rest of you as big?

danny: i'll tell you if i can get a copy of the book.

attendant: i also have a fine assortment of racy magazines that might interest *monsieur.*

danny: no, just *l'inferno* thanks.

(the attendant runs off to look for the book. beatrice enters the store. she wears shades and a scarf tied in a parisian style. her accent is unmistakably american.)

beatrice: jules!

(jules, the attendant calls from behind the store.)

attendant: hold the horses. i am trying to seduce the american.

beatrice: *(to danny)* that must be you, right?

danny: how did you know?

beatrice: it's obvious. you look american. you put your hands in your pockets like an american. you even smell like an american. i smelled your stench the minute i came into the store. american!

danny: i know you.

beatrice: don't get any wild ideas, buddy. just cause i'm also a yankee. just cause i stink of barbeques and fourth of july doesn't mean you know me at all. got it?

(the attendant returns with the inferno*)*

attendant: *(to danny.)* here you are, sexy. *(to beatrice.)* you look the scary little bitch today, *ma chère.* where did you get that scarf?

beatrice: it's a fake *hermés.*

attendant: *mon dieu!*

beatrice: hey! not just anyone can pull off fake *hermés* so give me some credit.

attendant: *pardon.* have you been practicing your *français?*

beatrice: i don't have time for a lesson. where's the stuff?

attendant: *(he runs behind the counter and fishes out a small paper bag.) voilà les madeleines.*

danny: madeleines*?*

beatrice: proust, honey. he takes a bite of that damn cookie, and vomits out a 5,000 page novel. try lifting that instead of a barbell. *(turns to jules.)* you're a queen among princesses, jules. *(she hands him a fistful of francs.)* i don't know what i'd do without you. *je me sais pas* or something like that. *adieu!*

(she exits.)

danny: who was she?

attendant: her name is beatrice. i do some favors for her. she sings at an underground club. *l'inferno.* just like your book.

(pause.)

danny: i'm supposed to meet a friend there, but he never told me where it was.

attendant: a rival! i should tie you up to keep you from running away.

danny: can you tell me how to get *l'inferno?*

attendant: i am powerless with you, my beautiful american. read to me from your book. titillate me with those kinky words of monsieur dante's.

danny: the book is about hell.

attendant: one man's hell is another's *champs elysees*. please, humor me. if you do, i'll tell you where this place is.

danny: do you promise?

attendant: i'll swear on anything you like.

danny: *(reading.)* *i am the way to the doleful city.*
i am the way into eternal grief.
i am the way to a forsaken race.

before me nothing but eternal things were made
and i shall last eternally.
abandon every hope, all you who enter.

(he stops.)

attendant: what's wrong?

danny: i know this. i've read these words before.

attendant: well, it's a famous book. read the rest. i'm very, very hard. i want you to pull me out right here in front of everyone. stroke me while you read your book.

danny: stop that!

attendant: don't spoil it, *cheri*. we're getting on so well!

danny: where is *l'inferno?*

attendant: i cannot let you go there.

danny: you promised me.

attendant: i cannot let you run to the arms of another. who is this man?

(silence.)

attendant: do you love him?

danny: he's waiting for me. he needs me to find him. tell me where it is.

attendant: let him wait. stay here with me. we'll have a drink. then we'll play satan and sinner.

danny: forget it. i'll find it myself.

attendant: and how will you do that?

(danny turns and sees magda staring at him through the window. she runs off.)

danny: i don't know. thanks for the book.

(he runs off.)

5.

(danny is running through paris. magda stands in front of notre-dame, reading a post card.)

magda: i am dreaming this dream.
i am running to the seine
and on *rue de rivoli*
i see a pizza place,
i see a coffee shop,
i see a deli,

and then they disappear.
i run past the *hôtel de ville*
and i see you by the carousel
but then i see the carousel is empty.
i am lost.
so i run to *notre dame.*
i run to the center of paris.
i run to figure out where i am.

(inside notre dame. *danny is reading the* inferno.*)*

danny: *i was among those dead who were suspended*
when a lady summoned me.
she was so blessed and beautiful,
i implored her to command me.
with eyes more bright than any star,
in low soft tones, she started to address me:
"i am beatrice, who urges you to go.
love moved me as it moved me now to speak."

(x appears.)

x: danny boy, look up at the stained glass.

danny: it's like the walls are made of glass. it's beautiful.

x: that's what the french want you to think. wanna know how many times this place has been practically destroyed? it's a skeleton. with stained glass skin. it's rotting. dissolving ...

(he vanishes. danny notices magda dipping her hand in the basin of holy water. she notices danny.)

danny: how's your son?

magda: he is ... fine.

danny: i've seen you twice.

magda: *que casualidad.*

danny: you're following me.

magda: *hijo, no!* i think you are too jetlagged. my son is very busy. he has things to do. i have to walk around alone.

danny: and do you have postcards of amnesia café and *les bon mots?*

magda: i was passing by. i saw you in the window.

danny: so why did you run away?

magda: i was ... embarrassed.

(she looks at her hand dripping holy water.)

magda: did you make the sign of the cross when you came in?

danny: i don't care about that stuff.

magda: *(putting her wet hand on his forehead.)* me neither. it's just a bad habit i have.

danny: it's cold.

magda: i'm sorry i scared you. i feel ... so scared here. my son has been too preocupado to notice me.

danny: and you came all this way to see him.

(danny tentatively puts his hand in hers.)

danny: i want you to look up.

(they are bathed in the light of one of the rosette windows.)

magda: it's like the most beautiful eye.

danny: it's an explosion.

(he closes his eyes.)

danny: i don't feel so good.

magda: *que te pasa, daniel?*

danny: *(opening his eyes. changing tone.)* did you know that during the nazi occupation, they took out all the stained glass windows and numbered each piece and filled the windows with sandbags?

magda: i cannot imagine. all those pieces of glass. to remember where they all go … i suppose if you love something, you remember.

danny: love? there have been so many times they've burned this church, ripped it apart. they said it was ugly. they took down the statues. they took down the gargoyles. so many people have wanted to tear it down, but they can't.

(they turn around and slowly walk towards the altar.)

magda: that's mary over there? on the altar?

danny: it's a *pieta.*

magda: it's disgusting, putting a woman holding a dead body in the middle of a church.

danny: that dead body is her son.

magda: it must have been sculpted by a man. only a man would find that beautiful. how would he know what it's like to watch your son die in front of you? to get his body back cold, lifeless … or worse … there is no body. he just disappears. there is no word. no nothing.

danny: i don't know if that's what's going on with mary.

magda: any time you lose someone … whether they die or they leave you, they just … disappear. it's the same. their eyes, their skin, their hands. their body breaks up into so many, many tiny pieces. they evaporate. and you try to remember, but you forget what their voice sounded like. you forget what they looked like when they cried and needed you to hold them. you forget their smile. you cannot remember something evaporated.

danny: if you love something, you remember.

magda: you're so young.

danny: i don't feel it.

(silence.)

magda: i have to apologize.

i have not been honest with you.

a couple weeks ago, i got a call from my son's landlord in new york. his rent was behind. it was the first i had heard of my son in a while. he never called. he ... he ... was not *discreto* with the kind of people he was dating. my husband wanted him out of the house. so he left school. he left miami and moved to new york.

i should have told him to stay. i should have stood up to my husband.

when his landlord called, i flew to new york right away. i went even though i was afraid of flying at the end of september. i was afraid to find out what had happened to my son. i went into his apartment. i looked through his things. clothes. pictures. postcards ... they were all from paris. they were addressed to someone else. some man. i read and read and read and i cried. his heart had broken. and after i finished reading, i thought, no i knew he was alright. he had just come back to paris, that's all. so i emptied my savings and paid his rent. i called my husband and told him i was going to find him.

i would be a different mother. i would not commit the same sin again.

danny: but you haven't found him?

magda: no. i didn't know how. but when i saw you and i thought ... i felt you could be like him and you could help me remember.

danny: i think ... i really think i am going crazy. people tell me i'm speaking french when i know i can't. i am getting calls on my cell phone even though i know that's impossible. i am starting to think maybe i should just go home. i just wish i had a different place to go home to.

magda: maybe that's what we both need. maybe we need to get back on the plane. maybe we need to go home and forget *esta locura*. and you know what else? we should eat something. are you hungry?

danny: i could be.

magda: i want to take you to lunch.

danny: yes. lunch and then back to the hotel. i can call the airline.

magda: there's a place my son mentions in his postcards. *l'inferno*.

(danny starts slightly.)

magda: what's the matter?

danny: what does your son say in the postcard?

magda: *(pulling out a postcard and reading.)* go for lunch. ask for a table.

there's an address here.

(danny examines the writing.)

danny: that's across the seine. i want to go.

magda: lead the way.

(the step outside. it is cold, rainy and windy.)

6.

(magda opens an umbrella. danny tenses.)

magda: get underneath the umbrella. you'll get sick, *hijo*.

danny: funny how spanish makes everyone related.

magda: you need a mother.

danny: you think so?

(lightning. danny tenses up.)

magda: now don't be afraid. we just need to cross the river and we'll be there in no time.

(they walk.)

magda: i am not used to walking so much. it's probably no problem for you living in new york, but in miami, well … you know … you drive around so much. it's so pretty here. *(she stops and stares at the seine.)* you stand on this bridge. right in the middle of this river. and you can see. you can make sense of everything. the buildings. the boats –

danny: *les bateaux mouche.*

magda: see, you can speak french.

danny: it was my ex. he knew everything. i just stood there. we were here last spring. and i got lost so many times. i was afraid to leave the hotel. i made him go everywhere and …

(his cellphone rings.)

magda: it's your phone.

danny: i'm afraid to answer it.

magda: who is it?

danny: him. he's been calling me. he knows i'm here.

magda: how?

danny: i don't know. i have to answer it. i have to talk to him. excuse me.

(he runs off down a side street.)

7.

(a side street. danny picks up the cell phone.)

x: you're shivering.

danny: where are you?

x: you're wet and cold.

danny: where is *l'inferno?* are you still there? tell me.

x: do you remember when we were walking to the eiffel tower and it suddenly began to rain? we didn't have our umbrellas and you were standing there with your arms crossed, soaking wet and frowning and i pulled you into me and held you there by the seine. do you remember what i said?

danny: please, stop doing this.

x: do you remember what i said?

danny: i want to hang up, but i can't.

x: i said, "this is how i want to always remember you."

danny: no. you didn't say anything.

x: i don't like how you're remembering this, danny. that isn't how it happened.

danny: you can't choose how you remember something.

x: don't you want to see me again, danny boy?

danny: don't ask me that.

x: isn't that why you came back to paris? i know how you're staying in the same room in the same hotel, eating in the same restaurants. you want to find me, don't you?

danny: no, i don't. i don't want to remember.

x: i want to see you. i came back and i can't remember my french. i can't read the maps. i can only remember you, danny boy. i can only remember you wet and shivering like you are now. find me, please.

danny: where are you?

(x hangs up.)

magda: daniel*!*

(magda runs over to danny.)

magda: look at you, you're soaking wet. we should go inside.

(she looks around. she takes out the postcard.)

magda: this is the street, but i don't see a sign.

(danny notices something on one of the doors.)

danny: *(reading.)* "abandon every hope, all you who enter." we're here.

magda: how do you know?

danny: i know.

(they open the door and step inside.)

8.

(they enter an impossibly small room, with one table and a small staircase in the rear, leading underground. the concierge from the hotel approaches danny and magda. the scene has a frenetic pace with the lines coming at a clip, almost overlapped.)

concierge: good afternoon.

danny: what are you doing here?

concierge: i work here, *monsieur.*

danny: you work at my hotel.

concierge: two for lunch?

danny: you told me you never heard of this place.

magda: is this the only table?

concierge: and a lovely one it is, *madame*, very clean.

danny: no, we want to go downstairs.

concierge: *madame*, your son is most rude.

danny: i'm not her son.

(kenny comes in the door. he and danny see each other.)

concierge: *(to kenny.)* good afternoon.

danny: *(to kenny.)* hey!

kenny: do i know you ... ?

(they stare at each other. the concierge runs over and breaks them up.)

concierge: *(to kenny.)* right this way, monsieur.

(the concierge grabs kenny.)

kenny: hey, wait a minute!

(the concierge shoves kenny down the staircase. danny runs after him. the concierge runs to the stairs, blocking danny's path.)

concierge: where do you think you're going?

magda: daniel, who was that? was that your ex?

danny: i am going downstairs.

concierge: behave yourself, *monsieur.*

danny: who the hell are you?

concierge: i am *le maitre d'hôtel* at *l'inferno, monsieur.*

danny: you are the concierge at the *hôtel de la bretonnerie.*

concierge: why would *monsieur* like to sit downstairs?

magda: i am staying at that hotel and i know he doesn't work there.

danny: *(to magda.)* you are?

magda: *(to danny.)* i have the top floor suite. *(to the concierge.)* what's downstairs?

concierge: *madame,* beatrice *la americaine* performs downstairs. there are some who like what she does and there are some who don't.

magda: what does she sing? french songs?

danny: jacques brel, right? she sings jacques brel.

concierge: ah, so you know brel? *are you sure you want to go downstairs?*

danny: yes.

magda: can we eat downstairs?

concierge: i will see what i can do about that, *madame.* now, if you will excuse me, i will see about a table.

(he exits down the stairs.)

danny: why didn't you tell me you are staying at that hotel?

magda: that's where my son liked to stay. he told me about it in a postcard.

danny: i want to see the postcards.

magda: they're mine. sit down and wait.

danny: i can't sit down. i can't do anything.

(he pulls out a cigarette and lights it.)

magda: you shouldn't smoke.

danny: you're not my mother, so stop it.

(the concierge emerges again. he walks past danny to magda.)

concierge: i have found a table. if i may escort *madame* first? it is a steep staircase.

magda: *merci.*

(she takes his hand and they descend the staircase. music. "ne me quitte pas." the concierge returns.)

concierge: *monsieur,* we are ready for you.

9.

(the concierge leads danny downstairs. they are in the middle of pere-lachaise. *among the graves, a small stage where beatrice is singing "if you go away," the official english translation of* "ne me quitte pas." *again, her manner is abstracted so she provides underscoring to the scene that follows. there is one café table near the stage and x is sitting at it. the concierge leads danny to the table.)*

beatrice: *if you go away*
on this summer day
then you might as well
take the sun away.
all the days that flew
in the summer sky
when our love was new
and our hearts were high
when the day was young
and the night was long
and the moon stood still
for the nightbird song.
if you go away …

concierge: here is your table, *monsieur.*

(he turns to leave.)

danny: wait, where's magda?

concierge: this is your table, *monsieur*. enjoy.

(he leaves.)

x: you are dreaming, danny boy.

danny: *(turning and noticing x.)* this is you, right? this is really you?

x: do you remember this song? do you remember what i told you?

danny: *it is necessary to forget.*

everything that has already flown
can be forgotten.
the times
filled with misunderstandings
the times lost
trying to understand
how to forget those hours
that kill the heart of happiness
with just a simple "why?"

x: do you remember what *"ne me quitte pas"* means?

danny: *don't leave me.*

x: don't leave me, danny boy.

(danny tries to reach out and touch x, but an arm pulls him back. it is the bookstore attendant. x vanishes.)

attendant: i told you not to come here.

danny: let go.

attendant: what do you think this is? you think you can do as you please? you think you can come into my store and insult me the way you did? let me tell you one thing. i lied to you. your french is abominable. pedestrian. you are a dumb, stupid, conceited american.

danny: i *understand* the words!

je ne vais plus pleurer
je ne vais plus parler
je me cacherai là
a te regarder
danser et sourire
et à t'écouter
chanter et puis rire
laisse-moi devenir
l'ombre de ton ombre
l'ombre de ta main

l'ombre de ton chien.

attendant: don't say that to me. don't claim you can speak the language when you are not sincere. don't claim your heart is broken, when you have stepped all over mine.

danny: i am dreaming ... i am dreaming ... i am dreaming.

attendant: are you, *mon beau garçon?* do people such as you dream? you with your perfect face, your dark eyes, your smooth skin ... you are marble. you don't dream.

(the attendant strikes danny hard across the face. danny drops to the floor.)

beatrice: *if you go away ...*
if you go away ...
if you go away ...

(beatrice's number is done. she bows as ghostly applause thunders throughout the tombs. darkness. after the applause dies down, the lights return. danny is crumpled on the floor and beatrice stands over him, holding two glasses of champagne.)

beatrice: jules can be such a shit.

danny: why didn't you stop him?

beatrice: i was singing. i don't stop for no one. besides, you reject jules, you deal with it. it's none of my business. i brought you something to drink.

danny: champagne?

beatrice: why not?

danny: my face feels broken.

beatrice: this is cheap champagne, but you'll feel better, trust me. you'll still look like shit, though. let me clean that up for you. hold these.

(she hands danny the glasses. she crouches down and undoes her scarf, which she dips in the champagne and tends to danny's face, which has some blood on it.)

danny: your *hermés.*

beatrice: they're buy one get one free on *rue de rivoli.*

danny: what is this place?

beatrice: *le cimitiere du pere-lachaise.* piaf is here. so is that fucker proust. but jules brought me here to see the americans. isadora. gertrude and alice. jim morrison. he said, "all good americans go to paris when they die."

danny: are you a good american?

beatrice: are you?

danny: i know you.

beatrice: from the bookstore. *les bons mots.*

danny: no, from new york.

beatrice: what book did you buy?

danny: dante's *inferno.*

(silence.)

beatrice: how do you like it?

danny: you've read it?

beatrice: gave it a read while jules was torturing me with colette. the french are fucking sadists i swear.

(she takes some pills.)

beatrice: how's your face?

danny: it stings.

beatrice: *(offering her pills.)* want one?

danny: will these kill me?

beatrice: very very slowly.

(danny takes a pill.)

danny: i want to leave.

beatrice: the cemetery is closed. you can't get out.

danny: that's impossible *(he looks around.)* i came in from over there … or was it over there?

beatrice: there is a lot you don't know about paris. you stay here long enough and you understand. things you begin to know.

danny: like what?

beatrice: i know you're staying at the *hôtel de la bretonnerie* because that's where you stayed with your ex last spring. i know you picked up some guy in amnesia café. i knew you were *in les bon mots* when i came in. i know your heart is like mine. broken.

(she presses her hand against his chest.)

beatrice: i can feel it. it's the same.

(she presses his hand against her chest.)

danny: why don't you remember meeting me in new york?

beatrice: there's a lot i don't remember. oh, i remember new york … or at least i try to.

danny: what do you see when you try?

beatrice: a window.

danny: a window?

beatrice: it was in some building. some tall building. i could look down onto streets. i remember they looked like perfect little squares. like you couldn't ever get lost down there. 90th floor. i remember i was on the 90th floor. looking out a window.

danny: were you at work?

beatrice: i think so. i remember a desk. pens. post-its. phone numbers on the post-its. "had fun last night. call me." piles of stuff. magazines. postcards of places i wished i could visit. window. looking out the window on the 90th floor. i remember that. i remember wanting to just step through the glass. to just fucking fly away, over those perfect little squares. to never get lost. i remember wishing this.

(she stops.)

danny: what?

beatrice: the sky …

danny: i'm sorry?

beatrice: the glass on the window. it *vanished.* and then there was sky. an incredibly blue and clear sky. that's all there was. my body and the sky. i was falling … i mean, no … i was … i was … *(this is very, very difficult.)* i want to say i was *flying.* i know that's impossible, ridiculous.

danny: maybe you dreamt it.

beatrice: no. it's the last thing i remember before … paris. i came to paris. i didn't remember buying a ticket or why i even decided to come. but here i am. and i can't go back. i don't know why. explain it to me. why aren't they letting people go back? did something happen?

(silence.)

beatrice: tell me!

danny: i'm sorry. i mean, i don't know. i'm clueless. so many weird things have happened to me and i can't explain anything.

beatrice: i can't call another airline to be told there are no flights. i can't find yet another door leading to a cemetery. i can't keep trying to find ways of killing myself. the pills don't work. the poisons aren't strong enough. the razor blades don't cut. i've been trying to remember. just like you. but my memories are all wrong. just like yours.

danny: my memories are fine.

beatrice: then why are you here? don't you see that if you remember, really remember, i will too. i know i will ... and then i'll know how i can go home again.

danny: how?

(she points to a set of stairs leading down.)

beatrice: just go down those stairs.

danny: what's there?

beatrice: it's the columbarium. it's where they keep the ashes of people who've been cremated. it's also where your memories are ... but only one of them is real.

(danny looks downstairs.)

danny: why don't you go down there yourself?

beatrice: when jules brought me here, he showed me this place. he said the same thing i said to you. i went down, but there was nothing. just walls of ashes.

danny: what if that's all there is? what if i go down there and nothing happens?

beatrice: let's just say i hope that doesn't happen

danny: me too

(he descends the stairs, his footsteps reverberating with each step.)

10.

(the columbarium. there are walls with plaques commemorating the ashes of each person stored inside. kenny stands by one of the walls.)

danny: what are you doing here?

kenny: i was looking at the p-p-plaques. smelling the roses people left. *in m-m-memoriam.*

danny: why did you act like you didn't know me?

kenny: there's so much about this place i d-d-don't understand. the night we met, when we fell asleep, i thought i had this dream. you and i fall in love. we go back to new york and move in together. you lie next to me and i can feel your fingers, your hands, your breath, c-c-cold, like ice. i hold you tighter, so i can warm you, but you are still cold. i ask you if you want to go to paris again, so we can remember how we m-m-met ... and we stay in the same room, trying to remember and one morning, a man comes up to me. "getting your sugar fix?" he says. i had no idea who he was. i never saw him before in my life. i run to the store i left you in, but you weren't there. and i realize that man was you. i didn't recognize you. i ran back, but you were g-g-g-gone. i ran around, trying to find you, but i couldn't remember what you looked like.

danny: i saw you this morning. you said you were at the *caron beaumarchais*. but we slept together at the *bretonnerie*.

kenny: did you leave this message?

(he turns on his cellphone and plays the message for danny. we hear it echo and amplified in the columbarium.)

danny's voice: help me kenny. i'm lost. i can't speak the language. i'm in *l'inferno.* find me.

danny: no. that's impossible. i didn't call you. my boyfriend. my ex-boyfriend called me. he asked me to find him. he asked me to go to *l'inferno.*

kenny: i don't believe you.

danny: this isn't happening. it. is. not.

(he tries to run back up the stairs. kenny grabs him.)

kenny: say you love me, danny boy. say it and believe it.

danny: how can i say i love you when all i remember is amnesia café?

kenny: you have to say it. you have to. i look at you and it's like i can't hold on to the image of your face. you're b-b-breaking apart. please … say it. stay with me.

danny: beatrice!

kenny: please?

danny: get off me!

kenny: don't let me go home alone, danny. don't … let me sleep alone. please …

danny: beatrice!

(the sound of heels coming down the stairs …)

danny: beatrice?

11.

(it is magda. danny runs to her as kenny vanishes.)

magda: daniel?

danny: oh, thank god! how did you get in? i want to leave. i want to go home ...

magda: daniel? is it really you?

danny: of course it is, c'mon let's go.

magda: i found these postcards and i knew ... i knew you would be here.

danny: no. you've got this all wrong.

magda: you don't remember me?

danny: you're the nice lady who sat next to me on the plane.

magda: i want to take you home.

danny: to new york?

magda: no, not there. it's not safe anymore. i want to take you back to miami. isn't that what you want? isn't that what you wrote here?

(she hands him a postcard.)

danny: *(reading) mami*, i'm at l'inferno. find me. take me home, please.

magda: it was delivered to the front desk at my hotel.

danny: i didn't write that.

magda: isn't that your handwriting? i know your handwriting. i remember.

danny: but, you're not my mother. no. my mother wouldn't come to paris by herself.

magda: you're bleeding.

danny: it's my lip. some guy hit me in l'inferno.

(magda comes over to him with a handkerchief. she cleans up the blood.)

magda: i see young men that could be your age and i ask myself, are his eyes like that? does he smile like that? every day that passes, your face becomes harder to hold in my mind. but, there must be something … some part of memory that can't be erased, hijo. you should remember me.

danny: i wish you were her. you almost made me forget what she was really like.

magda: it's better if you forget. i want to it to be different. i want to be a different mother to you. come home with me, please.

danny: i want to go someplace better. a city that didn't smell of burning. where all the buildings that have been destroyed have been built again.

magda: and here you are surrounded by walls of ashes. forget him.

danny: do you think i can?

magda: of course. it will be like he never existed. and then you can be happy.

(she extends her hand. we hear "ne me quitte pas.")

magda: come home, daniel.

(x appears behind danny.)

x: danny boy.

danny: *(reciting.)* *ne me quitte pas*
il faut oublier
tout peut s'oublier
qui s'enfuit déjá

magda: *dame la mano, daniel, y olvidate.*

danny: *oublier le temps*
des malentendus
et le temps perdu
a savoir comment

x: *(extending his hand.)* take my hand, danny boy.

danny: *oublier les heures*
qui tuaient parfois
a coups de pourquoi
le coeur du bonheur

(to magda.) i can't.

(danny takes x's hand. magda vanishes.)

12.

x: what does "ne me quitte pas" mean?

danny: don't leave me.

x: you've learned.

danny: am i dreaming?

x: you are remembering.

danny: but i came here to forget.

x: you came here to remember, but you can't choose what you remember. turn around

(there is a wall behind them filled with flyers of missing persons.)

x: this is what you've come back to.

danny: this isn't new york.

x: it's a room of ashes. it might as well be new york. look at the flyers.

(danny notices the same picture of beatrice from the subway station in new york. it speaks:)

beatrice: my name is beatrice. i worked on the 90th floor. i do not smile. i stare at you cold. hard. i am remembering. tuesday. something is wrong. i don't want to be a secretary this morning. do not want to be here. in this conference room, staring out the window … i am remembering. the glass. vanishing. the sky. the incredibly blue and clear sky. i am remembering why i can't go home.

danny: i saw her in new york. in the subway station … or did i?

x: what were you remembering?

danny: it was her.

x: the woman at the bar? the sad french woman, lost and heartbroken in new york, city of death?

danny: i didn't mean to look. i didn't want to look.

x: why did you keep calling me?

danny: why did you tell me you were here?

x: it's what you wanted to believe. it was what you would rather remember than realize it wasn't that woman you were looking for in the flyers. it was me, danny boy.

danny: no, it wasn't.

x: this is the true memory. this is it. look.

(x holds out a flyer with a picture of himself.)

danny: i won't … i'm not going to remember that.

x: you're not going to remember me?

(silence.)

x: answer me.

(silence.)

x: i am evaporating, danny.

danny: exploding.

x: i wanted to see you. i wanted you to say, "i love you" to me.

danny: i … can't. *(he is crying.)* i want to go home. i want you to come home with me.

x: danny boy, please.

(he holds out the flyer once more. danny takes it and really looks at it.)

danny: i … love … you.

x: i love you, too.

danny: but what does it matter? i still have to go back to my apartment alone. i love you doesn't mean anything anymore.

x: it means something to me. thank you.

(he turns to go.)

danny: *ne me quitte pas.*

x: it will get better. i promise.

(there is a roar. x vanishes. beatrice is revealed sobbing on the floor. danny runs over to her and grabs her hand. the roar gets louder. it is the sound of a subway. danny closes his eyes and shuts his ears. blackout.)

13.

(on the n train, new york city. danny opens his eyes. a woman dressed in red sits next to him, disheveled.)

woman: *(singing.)*
ne me quitte pas (don't leave me.)
je t'inventerai (i will invent)
des mots insensés (senseless words)
que tu comprendas (that you will understand)
je te parlerai (i will speak about)
de ces amants lá (those lovers who)
qui ont vu deux fois (have seen their)
leurs couers s'embraser (hearts embrace twice)
je te raconterai (i will tell you)
l'histoire de ce roi (the story of a king)
mort de n'avoir pas (who died because)
pu te recontrer. (he wasn't able to see you again.)

danny: i know that song.

woman: jacques brel.

danny: don't leave me.

woman: that's it. do you speak french?

danny: no. it's just that that song reminds me of someone.

woman: it's such a sad song.

danny: you look familiar to me.

woman: really? where do you remember me from?

danny: you just look like someone i met in paris.

woman: paris … i have dreams about paris.

danny: so do i. i was just there.

woman: please tell me it was romantic.

danny: i just needed to leave new york.

woman: and are you glad to be back?

(silence. the train stops.)

danny: this is my stop. thanks for the brel, *merci beaucoup.*

woman: *de rien, monsieur.*

(danny turns to the open door of the train. the woman takes out some pills and puts them in her mouth. danny steps out of the train … end of play.)

marea
a play by alejandro morales

originally commissioned by the joseph papp public theater/new york
shakespeare festival, george c. wolfe, producer. subsequent workshop at
new dramatists/playtime.

characters:

maria: her eyes and hair are dark. she is obsessed with post war italian cinema, particularly that of the late 50s-early 60s and dresses in a manner similar to italian movie stars of this period. her manner is precise, exact. she suffers from asthma.

claudia/monica: two women played by the same actress. she is the same age as maria. claudia is a new york intellectual that seems uncomfortable in the monica vitti veneer she wears. monica, on the other hand, does a great monica vitti impression. she is fabulous, theatrical and sports a european air.

regla: maria's grandmother. she is a catholic hypochondriac, yet she is a woman with steely emotions and convictions. if she seems exaggerated, she would tell you she has good reason to be.

caridad: maria's mother. she appears in the guise of a b-movie villainess/ghost in the manner of italian gothic horror diva, barbara steele. a dark, exotic beauty.

"how does one define a cult film? there are certain cohesive ingredients. cult films usually have an element of unease - *ana*rchy, transgressing certain taboos; they are almost always excessive and camp and speak to the counterculture. certainly, most have an aura of irreverence, and are usually made on low budgets, therefore requiring a certain energized spontaneity, somewhat like graffiti. after all, film is so porous, and to my mind, so oddly occult, that i think that film itself absorbs odd energies like a living skin.
– barbara steele
"cult memories"

on style:

what attracted me to italian horror was the way these films could oscillate from sheer ridiculousness to lyricism while maintaining a certain integrity. later, while watching martin scorcese's *my voyage to italy*, i was struck by his comment that humor and pathos were equally present in many of the great post-war italian films. this play was written in that vein. while there should be great care to play these characters honestly, one should not do this at the expense of the elements melodrama and camp written into the script. work to find a way to make both exist. a contemporary (albeit non italian) example can be found in the films of pedro almodóvar.

part one

1.

(maria, in her living room. there is a door to a bathroom and a door to a bedroom, but maria is standing by a third door. her relationship to the door is one part incredible fear and one part insatiable desire. she runs her hands over the door. silence. she tries the doorknob.)

maria: make it turn ... make it turn.

(it does not open. silence. there is whispering behind the door. she steps away. the whispering becomes more distinct:)

voice: fade in ...

(the doorknob begins to turn on its own. it begins to rattle. someone is trying to get out.)

voice: fade in ...

(maria is about to scream, but she can't. she steps away from the door. the doorknob rattles wildly.)

voice: *siete la mia vittima. sono venuto esigerla.*

(claudia appears dressed in some chic sixties garb holding a blonde wig.)

claudia: is this what you wanted?

(the rattling stops. maria composes herself.)

maria: *che stupenda! (she looks at claudia.)* let's play.

2.

(the scene is set for a photo session. a hasselblad camera on a tripod, lighting, etc. various file folders with black and white film stills are arranged on a table nearby.)

maria: today we're doing monica vitti in *l'avventura.* i pulled some stills from my files. *(she grabs one.)* this is the face i want. see here. monica– that is, *her character, claudia*–is resisting the advances of sandro played by ... ?

claudia: gabrielle ferzetti.

maria: *brava.* now. the face. she looks off into the distance. she will not look at him. she can't. if she does, she is done for. got it? good. let's go.

(claudia puts on the wig. she sits down with the still and emulates the face. maria walks over to her camera and photographs her.)

claudia: i am teaching *l'avventura* this semester, you know.

maria: i've noticed the dvd's misplaced.

claudia: i hate *l'avventura.*

maria: you like *l'avventura.*

claudia: it feels like drowning.

maria: the eyes. look away. off in the distance. why teach it if you hate it?

claudia: the island sequence. the bit with lea masari–

maria: –anna ...

claudia: she and sandro are chatting it up, you know, *having the talk.* and she tells sandro she's grown "used to being alone." and she's like this fury trapped inside the body of this ordinary woman. her hair whips around in the wind and she's like fire only she's surrounded by all this water and the waves are crashing all around her ... and *anna* will be extinguished. you just know.

maria: resist. no desire. no giving in.

claudia: i used to think you looked like lea masari.

maria: and i don't anymore?

claudia: would you do what she did? disappear on an island, vanish into thin air? just like that?

maria: say, *"diame un bacio."*

claudia: dah-meh oon bah-chee-oh.

maria: *bah-cho.*

claudia: bah-cho.

maria: *che donna bella sei.*

claudia: say that in spanish.

maria: hold it. right there. yes. resist. *(she shoots.)* perfect.

claudia: kiss me.

(maria steps away from behind the camera. she walks over to claudia.)

maria: *bellisima.*

claudia: can i take off the wig?

maria: leave it.

(maria kisses claudia's neck, claudia looks away ala monica vitti, resisting and then giving in. as the kissing intensifies, blackout.)

3.

maria: the dream always plays out the same way. me running through this house. don't recognize said house, but it's got halls that go on for days. endless. there's someone ahead of me. someone in the shadows. i run after her, but no matter how fast i run, i can never seem to catch up. and then ... see this: in this house, something happens. the halls are filling up with water. i can't run. i trip. i scrape myself. blood pouring into the water which by now is up to my waist. i cannot run anymore and i sense someone is behind me. i turn and all i see is a black glove. and a razor. that's it.

4.

(maria and claudia. claudia is in another dress, holding another wig.)

maria: monica vitti again today. this time *l'eclisse.*

claudia: the wig looks the same.

maria: she has more of a flip in *l'ecclise.* look here. *(she holds up a still.)* flip.

claudia: what are you going to do with all these photos?

maria: don't know. but it's about time i got serious about pictures again. i'm thirty. i have to find the thing, that *one real thing* ...

(she pauses for a moment ... then back on track.)

maria: now. this is the face. monica and alain delon. delon is kissing monica. his head buried in her neck and she is ecstatic, because, well, he's alain delon. eyes half closed, chin tilted up like so. see? okay. let's go.

(claudia studies the still, emulating the face. maria walks behind her camera.)

maria: ready?

claudia: *diame un bacio*

maria: put the wig on.

(claudia puts the wig on and sits for the camera. maria begins to shoot.)

claudia: i read something interesting today.

maria: what's that?

claudia: one of my students. they cited a source in their midterm paper about antonioni. "the director gazed at things radically, to the point of their exhaustion. this is dangerous. to look longer than is required disturbs any established order."

maria: the eyes. look over there. *(claudia averts her gaze accordingly.)* do you think that's true? to look at something too much is dangerous?

claudia: it's the way you look at it.

maria: move your shoulder towards me. is this going in your book?

claudia: i haven't decided.

maria: raise your chin. there you go. say, *"state transformandome."*

claudia: i like the way you say it better.

maria: very well. *state transformandome.*

claudia: *grazie.*

maria: *desidero un bacio.*

monica: *baciame.*

(maria kisses claudia's neck. claudia tosses her head back.)

maria: *te adoro ... monica ...*

claudia: *claudia.*

maria: *siete monica.*

(claudia pulls away.)

claudia: i am not monica.

maria: fine. claudia. come back here.

claudia: no.

maria: fine. we're done for today.

(she begins to put away her equipment.)

maria: at least i got some good shots.

claudia: *cara*, i'm sorry but–

maria: –i'm busy.

claudia: i'm worried.

maria: yes, me too. so do me a favor and open that bottle of chianti i brought home. let's at least be drunk while we *worry.*

claudia: chianti?

maria: this one is supposed to be good. voluptuous.

claudia: voluptuous …

(silence.)

claudia: she called again.

maria: who did?

claudia: your grandmother.

maria: what did the old vampire have to say?

claudia: she knows you're avoiding her.

maria: she's right. the chianti, if you don't mind.

claudia: i don't know why you bother with photography when denial is clearly your talent.

maria: repeat that, please?

claudia: chianti. nice, voluptuous chianti.

(claudia sets about opening the bottle.)

maria: what's this about? you want to meet grandma? you're curious, are you?

claudia: no, this isn't about–

maria: –she's as horrible as i say she is. completely.

claudia: what makes her so horrible?

maria: *(cutting herself on her equipment.)* dammit! i'm bleeding.

claudia: your grandmother has to know something. maybe she'll tell you now that you're older.

maria: there's nothing to tell. my mother's probably dead.

(claudia extends her hand to maria.)

claudia: *cara.*

maria: don't do that.

claudia: what's the matter?

maria: claudia, for godssake, will you finish pouring the chianti?

(claudia hands her a glass. they drink in silence.)

maria: it's not bad, is it?

claudia: i hate chianti.

maria: you like chianti.

claudia: no. i *fucking* hate chianti.

maria: but this is really good. can't you *see* that?

claudia: i hate to break this to you, but i'm not an idiot.

maria: you may have a couple of degrees, but what the hell are you ever going to do with them?

claudia: i like teaching.

maria: you should make films.

claudia: i don't want to make films.

maria: but that would be *something, cara*, something great!

claudia: like these photos of yours?

maria: okay, forget this. i can find another model.

claudia: this morning i had to think twice before i could use the dental floss. i couldn't get my contacts in on the first try. i put my right foot in my left shoe. *this is my life.* if i was going to get these basic things together, i would have by now.

maria: you know, i thought you would be happy to help me with this project. i thought it would be fun for you to play the movie star.

claudia: i don't need to play the movie star. i happen to find my orgy of fuck-ups charming. they make me distinct. something you don't have to worry about coming from where you come from.

maria: where i come from?

claudia: you have a genetic advantage. your family dealt with communism. mine dealt with coupons and casseroles.

maria: now you are boring me.

claudia: i'm sorry i don't *fascinate* you.

maria: where i come from is provincial same as any other place is provincial.

claudia: since when is miami provincial?

maria: it's filled with conservative, old world people who can't speak english and lack any sort of breeding or class. period. full stop. end of story.

claudia: you have no clue. even your language is more interesting. it's juicy. all those vowels are like big, wet gaping orifices. why don't you ever speak spanish to me?

maria: spanish fatally infected me and i've spent my entire life trying to recover.

claudia: so italian is a halfway home for romance language recovery?

maria: that's different.

claudia: tell that to my folks in iowa. spanish or italian. juicy is juicy and they don't grow juicy in iowa.

maria: of course they do, *cara.*

claudia: oh wait, was that a *compliment?*

maria: forget iowa. where you come from is not as important as where you end up. all successful people are essentially escape artists. chameleons. the past is only there to forget and you, *cara,* are forgetting that little midwestern hamlet for good.

claudia: sometimes i feel you would have nothing to do with me if i didn't share a name with monica vitti's character in *l'avventura*.

maria: why are you insecure? why do you think i don't love you?

claudia: i'm afraid.

maria: what can you possibly have to be afraid of? what is there to be afraid of when there's wine? women?

(she starts up the cd player.)

maria: and song?

(a jaunty bit of nino rota film music comes on. maria dances around claudia working her wine glass and a cigarette as props.)

maria: and ciggies of course. where would we be without ciggies? those plumes of smoke? sooooooo *via veneto*, 1960.

(she extends her hand.)

maria: dance with me.

(claudia tentatively takes her hand. the dancing becomes less rhythmic and more sensuous and sloppy. claudia embraces maria. the door from the top of the play opens a crack and a black glove wielding a straight razor appears in the crack. maria stiffens.)

claudia: *cara?* what's wrong? *cara?*

maria: i ... *can't breathe. (panic.)* i can't breathe ... help me ... *cara!*

5.

(the scene shifts. claudia disappears. maria is alone. from behind the door, we hear a voice:)

voice: *siete la mia vittima. sono venuto esigerla.*

(the hand with the razor retreats. the door continues to open revealing a beautiful woman around maria's age. she is dressed impeccably, circa thirtysomething years ago. she advances slowly.)

woman: you have been running.
you have been trying to escape.
hand on doorknob
after doorknob.
but one morning,
as you run,
you are faced with a doorknob
that doesn't turn
and you notice
one, lone drop of water.
small, simple and clear.
an exquisite jewel,
slowly sliding down the door,
onto the knob of the door
that seems familiar
and it hits you.
you have been running but
haven't gone anywhere at all.

maria: who are you?

(the woman grabs maria, pinning her to the wall, pressing herself against her.)

woman: the morning light
erupts through the window.
the light catches
the pearly drops,
sliding down the door
to the knob of the door
in your apartment.
the one that never opens.
and you notice your hand has become wet.
you notice the water,
your palm,
in the morning light,

has turned red,
deep red.

maria: stop it! i can't breathe.

(the woman raises the razor. maria is paralyzed.)

woman: it becomes clear.
it becomes obvious.
you cannot run.
you cannot escape.
you can close your eyes,
shutting the lids tightly,
but even then,
the darkness is stained burgundy.
it becomes clear
it becomes obvious.
inevitable.
i will claim you.

(she runs the dull side of the blade over maria's body. it does not cut. the gesture is sensual and maria almost swoons.)

maria: tell me who you are. please.

(claudia appears.)

claudia: *cara?*

(the woman releases maria and retreats towards the door. the scene shifts to:)

6.

maria: my bag! get me my bag!

(claudia grabs the bag and hands it to maria. maria pulls out an inhaler. she takes a hit.)

claudia: what's going on?

maria: asthma … i've been getting attacks again … it's like …

claudia: i didn't know you had asthma.

maria: … i felt trapped … everything was …

claudia: you shouldn't be smoking.

maria: i shouldn't be doing a lot of things. (her breath resumes.) i'm fine. really

claudia: you sure?

maria: i just haven't been sleeping well.

(she goes over to the door.)

maria: do you know what's behind there?

claudia: supposedly this apartment and the one next door used to be one large unit.

maria: who lives there?

claudia: i think it's vacant now. the super says it's cursed. they can't keep the place occupied. apparently several years ago the woman who lived there died in the apartment. inez upstairs says she was stabbed to death, but the super says it was suicide. she slashed her wrists. he was the one who found her. but inez swears she heard screams.

maria: i hear things …

claudia: *(excited.)* oh my god, really?

maria: maybe i dreamt them. i've been having nightmares.

claudia: too much espresso.

maria: a hand in a black glove. straight razor. blood.

claudia: you're kidding! it's like a *giallo!*

maria: *giallo?*

claudia: italian slasher flicks. i've been doing research.

maria: research?

(silence.)

claudia: i didn't want to say anything because i wasn't sure yet, but ... i've been working my way through some italian horror films. i'm thinking there might be a book there.

maria: b-movies? what's wrong with antonioni? or even fellini?

claudia: everyone writes about antonioni and fellini.

maria: visconti?

claudia: italian horror is sexy. look at these.

(she produces an envelope.)

claudia: that kid at kim's video found them for me at a convention.

maria: *a convention?*

claudia: isn't she amazing?

(she pulls out the photos. they are of barbara steele.)

maria: oh, god, that's barbara steele! she had a tiny part in *8 ½*.

claudia: she's the queen of italian horror. *(she hands maria the photos.)* that one is from *terror creatures from beyond the grave. (another photo.)* that's *the ghost* or *lo spettro* in italian. *(another photo.) the faceless* *monster*, which is fabulous. *(another photo.)* and this … this is my favorite. *black sunday* or *la maschera del demonio*.

maria: your accent is pathetic.

claudia: *(lighting a cigarette. vampish.)* *non sei potuto resisterme.*

maria: barbara steele, huh?

claudia: you need to see *la maschera del demonio*. barbara steele's family is under the curse of this evil vampire, also played by barbara steele. when they killed her they nailed this mask to her face. that's why she has all these holes in her skin …

maria: *(muttered.)* curses and vampires.

(as claudia keeps talking about la maschera del demonio, *time shifts. regla, maria's grandmother appears holding a broken statue of* la caridad del cobre. *the scene should feel dubbed or subtitled.)*

7.

maria: *no puedo respirar.* (i can't breathe.)

regla: *maria, eso te pasa por ser atrevida.* (maria, that's what you get for being where you shouldn't.)

maria: *abuela, no fue mi culpa. tropese.* (grandmother, it wasn't my fault. i tripped.)

regla: *esta estatua de la caridad vino de cuba y me la rompiste.* (this statue of our lady of charity came from cuba and you broke it.)

maria: *perdoname.* (forgive me.)

regla: *no me pidas perdón a mi. pideselo a la virgen.* (don't ask me for forgiveness. ask the virgin.)

maria: *me duele el pecho.* (my chest hurts.)

regla: *pidele perdón a la virgen.* (ask the virgin for forgiveness.)

claudia: *cara?*

(regla disappears. maria uses her inhaler.)

claudia: are you listening to me?

maria: i need to take a bath.

claudia: you think this book is a bad idea.

maria: no. i just … i had my heart set on antonioni. excuse me.

claudia: maria, *cara …*

(maria closes the door behind her.)

claudia: *(under her breath.)* fuck you.

(darkness. sound of water running.)

8.

(the darkness is broken by flickering black and white imagery from la maschera del demonio.*)*

claudia: the doctors enter the family crypt. it's dark, dusty. the bowels of moldavia. and then the doctors see the coffin. they have to. in movies like this, it stands to reason. the things normal people do everything in their power to avoid are objects of attraction in a horror film. people are drawn closer, possessed, even though they should know better. they get nearer to the coffin, which has a cross and a window on the lid. through the window, you can see barbara steele. princess asa. a vampire. a witch. and it's like we have no choice but to look, even though we know we shouldn't. we can't help it. the camera is sucked under the surface. under the glass.

(maria appears floating amidst the images from la maschera del demonio. *the woman appears.)*

woman: fade in:
underwater.
it is very, very dark.
you are afraid.
you can't see.
you can't identify
any shadow,
any shade of black
swimming and surrounding you,
caressing you,
slow and silent silk.

cut to:

claudia: princess asa is wearing the mask of satan. *la maschera del demonio.* as punishment for her sins, it was nailed to her face. "her true face," they call it.

woman: cut to:
my approach.
and you sense me
coming nearer and nearer.
i come to claim you.
i am pure stealth,
precise,
perfect,
pristine,
premeditated.
my return,
here at the bottom of the ocean,
has been infinitely planned.

(she grabs maria. it is unclear whether the gesture is meant to smother or embrace.)

woman: the air drains from your lungs.
there is burning behind your breast.

maria: let go of me!

woman: you are suffocating.

maria: why are you doing this?

woman: you cannot resist.
you must give in.

claudia: one of the doctors is attacked by a bat. the cross over the coffin is smashed and it breaks the glass surface.

woman: the drowning girl pulls the victim down.

claudia: the doctors hands are reaching under, prying the mask of satan from asa's face. her true face.

maria: *(realizing.)* your face. i know your face.

(the woman lets maria go.)

woman: what did you just say?

(maria touches the woman's face.)

maria: i know you from somewhere … this is the face.

woman: this isn't what happens. this isn't in the script.

maria: what script?

claudia: asa's face is like a mannequin's. smooth. perfect, except she's missing her eyes.

woman: fade in. exterior. the ocean is a sheet of glass.

claudia: her skin, like glass.

maria: i've seen this.

woman: and then we see an arm cutting through the surface. just the arm. and then the waves grow.

maria: i know this movie. it was … it was … it scared me, i remember.

woman: you need to stop being afraid and learn to drown. follow the script.

maria: but i don't want to drown.

claudia: her body is preserved … it has not forgotten itself.

woman: it doesn't matter whether you do or you don't. that's what he wrote.

maria: who did?

woman: *el italiano.*

maria: *el italiano?*

woman: he wrote the part for me. i am the drowning girl and you are my victim. see?

(the woman pulls out the razor.)

maria: no! don't!

claudia: the doctor has cut his hand on the broken glass.

woman: you must stop resisting. just give in to me. give in.

claudia: there is enough blood. just a couple drops, which we see in close up, dripping down.

(the woman takes the razor to maria's leg and cuts. maria exhales sensuously. the woman is taken aback by the unexpected reaction.)

maria: i can breathe. i can really breathe.

woman: marea?

claudia: there is just enough blood to drip into asa's hollowed eye sockets. just enough to revive her as this dark, black fluid begins to rise inside her skull.

(blackout.)

9.

(maria steps out of the bathroom. claudia is sitting in the dark staring out the window.)

maria: claudia ...

claudia: i was sitting here thinking. asking myself why. you think you're safe. you think everything is going to work out and then one day the thread your entire life hangs by just snaps. and you can't explain why that is. shit happens. someone slashes your throat. tough luck. the end.

maria: come to bed.

claudia: i'm going to sleep on the couch.

maria: there's absolutely no reason for this.

claudia: no there's absolutely no reason. are you done in the bathroom?

(she heads over to the bathroom. on the way she notices a photograph on the floor. she looks at it and hands it to maria.)

claudia: this one is yours.

(maria looks at the photograph. she gasps.)

maria: where did you get this picture?

claudia: it fell on the floor. you must have dropped it when you were taking out your monica vitti collection.

maria: this is the mediterranean.

claudia: from our trip? you said the film was ruined.

maria: it wasn't. i never developed the film. i just had a crazy idea to walk into the ocean with my camera photographing the waves. i was almost underwater. i almost dr–... i almost ruined the camera. *(she notices something in the photo.)* oh, god! look at this picture.

(she shows claudia the photo.)

maria: see here. right here.

claudia: it's a fish or a bird or something.

maria: it's an arm. someone is drowning in this photo.

claudia: see this is exactly what i'm talking about. there's no arm there. look i don't know what's going on, but we need to talk, *cara*, we can't keep going on like... *(she stops. she notices a trickle of blood on maria's leg)* you're bleeding.

maria: what?

claudia: on your leg. what happened?

maria: i cut myself shaving.

claudia: let me see that.

maria: *(grabbing some tissue and wiping her leg.)* it's ... nothing.

(claudia takes off for the bathroom closing the door behind her. maria chases after her, but too late.)

maria: claudia?

(time shifts. regla appears holding the broken statue. the scene has the same dubbed/subtitled quality.)

10.

maria: *no puedo respirar.* (i cannot breathe.)

regla: *trate de arreglar la virgen.* (i tried to fix the virgin.)

maria: *llama al doctor.* (call the doctor.)

regla: *la goma no trabajo.* (the glue didn't work.)

maria: *llama al doctor.* (call the doctor.)

regla: *es tu culpa, maria.* (it's your fault, maria.)

maria: *¿que le paso a mi mamá? ¿dondé esta?* (what happened to my mother? where is she?)

regla: *es tu culpa, maria.* (it's your fault, maria.)

(the door of the bathroom flies open. claudia storms in. regla disappears.)

11.

(claudia produces a razor blade wrapped in bloody tissues.)

claudia: what's this doing in the wastebasket?

maria: so you've found out.

claudia: why are you doing this again?

maria: i'm fine! i've got everything under control!

claudia: take off your robe!

maria: leave me alone!

claudia: i said take it off!

maria: fine.

(maria parts her robe and shows claudia her legs. they have multiple cuttings on them. claudia looks away.)

maria: look at me! you wanted to see didn't you?

claudia: what's gotten into you?

maria: you and your little movies. the black glove. the razor.

claudia: you know, this is really sad. it's pathetic and it's disgusting.

maria: it disgusts you? well, it serves you right. when it's fucking barbara steele with holes all over her face, when it's in a movie it's art, it's amazing, it's the subject of a goddamn book.

claudia: you are ridiculous. i'm not the one running around collecting wigs and dresses to match the film stills in your collection. i'm not the one who said, "you'd look better as a blonde, claudia." "wear this dress, claudia," "smoke these cigarettes, claudia." "drink chianti. you like chianti." and nothing i say, nothing i do … i hate living here with you! i hate everything about it!

(she opens up a closet and pulls out a slew of vintage dresses and wigs. she violently throws them at maria.)

claudia: i am not monica vitti. i am not sophia loren. i am not even anna fucking magnani.

maria: you're the one who wants to be exciting. voluptuous, juicy. these dresses. these wigs. those stills are the most beautiful things i own. i wanted to help you.

claudia: is that what you really want?

maria: i want to make you happy. i want to take care of you.

claudia: i don't know why since you despise me so much.

maria: i don't despise you.

claudia: do you love me?

maria: i want you to love me.

claudia: what if i didn't speak italian? if i drank something other than chianti? if my hair was brown again?

maria: i just want to be here with you. please.

claudia: too late. i think you should leave.

maria: but this is my home.

claudia: no, maria, this is my home and i don't think you belong here anymore.

(maria strikes claudia. claudia strikes her back. silence. claudia walks out. maria collapses on the pile of dresses and wigs.)

12.

maria: monica ...

(nino rota plays. monica appears. she very much looks the part of a 60s european film star, or someone who'd very much like to be one. she wears shades, smokes cigarettes and vamps around. note: her dialogue is taken from the faceless monster.*)*

maria: monica, is it you?

monica: "yes it's my flesh. the flesh you thought was destroyed. but you can't destroy flesh. any more than you can destroy love or hate. it's the same thing."

maria: i need you to help me. come back to me.

monica: "you gave me extreme pleasure. you taught me the torment of the flesh, which turns into ecstasy that passes from life into death and receives eternity. now i'm going to reward you with that same pleasure. come, darling."

maria: have you forgotten me? i'm afraid.

monica: "don't be afraid. i'll stay with you and my body and my senses until someone comes and destroys my heart."

maria: take off your sunglasses. let me look at your face.

(she removes the shades. monica removes her wig, revealing claudia underneath.)

maria: claudia? what's happening?

(claudia extends her hands. she puts on black gloves.)

claudia: "scream, curse, beg. now i've got your body and your monstrous soul if there's anything in your damn being. it's my moment now."

(claudia grips maria's throat.)

claudia: remind yourself
what you believe in.
photographs are not real.
movies are not real.
memories are not real.
because you see,
because you watch,
because you remember
does not make it so.

(maria escapes from claudia's grip. she runs to the unopenable door. it flies open and regla appears holding the broken statue.)

regla: *desgraciada. malagradecida. asquerosa. pidele perdon a la virgen.*
(miserable. ungrateful. filthy. ask the virgin for forgiveness.)

maria: i can't breathe … i can't breathe …

regla: *que hiciste, maria?* (what have you done, maria?)

maria: *fue un accidente.* (it was an accident.)

(the woman enters. she stands behind regla. she will translate regla's dialogue, but as she translates, her delivery becomes more and more sincere.)

regla: *esta estatua me recuerda de tu mamá.*

woman: this statue reminds her of your mother.

regla: *yo le pedi …*

woman: and she begged …

regla: *le rese a la caridad del cobre …*

woman: she prayed …

regla: *por una hija.*

woman: she prayed for a daughter.

regla: *pero no salía en estado.*

woman: she couldn't get pregnant.

regla: *y le ofrecí hasta mi propia vida …*

woman: she offered her life …

regla: *pero nada. trate de olvidarme.*

woman: she tried to forget, but …

regla: *pero día tras día un dolor en mi vientre.*

woman: there was a pain in her womb. like a fist.

regla: *como un puño. y le dije a la virgen que se vaya para el carajo.*

woman: she told the virgin to go to hell.

regla: *ella que fue dichosa. elegida.*

woman: what did the virgin know? the virgin had been fortunate. she had been chosen.

regla: ella no comprendía este dolor.

woman: the virgin didn't understand this pain.

regla: *¡vete para el carajo, le dije!*

woman: she told her to go to hell and then …

regla: *salí en estado.*

woman: she was pregnant.

regla: *tu abuelo estaba orgulloso, pero yo tuve miedo.*

woman: your grandfather was happy, but she … she was afraid.

regla: *mi furia, mis palabras agitaron la virgen y pensé que me haya maldecido.*

woman: her fury, her words angered the virgin and she thought the virgin had cursed her.

regla: *pero el parto fue bueno, y mi hija bella.*

woman: the birth went well and she … she found me beautiful.

regla: beautiful.

woman: *la felicidad le vino a los treinta años, por fin.*

regla: happiness came to me at thirty. finally.

woman: *esos ojitos negros como asabaches.*

regla: those little black eyes, like onyxes.

woman: *me llamó caridad para que la virgen no me dañara.*

regla: i named her caridad so the virgen wouldn't hurt her.

caridad: *me llamó caridad para que yo fuera dichosa. elegida.*

regla: i named her caridad so she would be fortunate. chosen.

caridad: and i was. *fui elegida.*

maria: and then what happened?

regla: you took her from me.

maria: how?

regla: she left because of you.

maria: i can't breathe.

regla: and now you've broken my statue.

maria: i'm being sucked back.

regla: her namesake and her memory ... broken. shattered.

maria: please, *abuela*, tell me what happened to her? where has she gone? i need to know.

regla: all you need to know is you are a poor excuse for a granddaughter.

(regla disappears, leaving maria and caridad alone.)

caridad: *ya sabes, marea.*

maria: repeat that.

caridad: *marea ...*

maria: that's not my name.

caridad: of course it is.

maria: you are not her.

caridad: who else would i be?

maria: you're not the way i imagined.

caridad: i am exactly how you remembered.

(she holds up the photograph of the ocean.)

caridad: how far into the ocean did you feel like walking that day? how much did you desire to submerge yourself? how intensely did you long for the silence below the surface?

maria: with all my heart ...

caridad: you felt compelled. possessed.

maria: it was irrational. all of this is irrational.

caridad: so many things are. the calling of one's blood. the alphabet of heartbeats and pulses. to thirst for salt. incomprehensible to others, even to yourself. but you thirst all the same.

maria: but you can resist. i resisted. i didn't drown.

caridad: you must have resisted quite a bit. the desire must have been strong enough to cause your eye to find this arm among the waves of the caribbean.

maria: that day ... the day i walked into the ocean, i was in italy. that was the mediterranean.

caridad: no. this is the caribbean. look at the color of the water.

maria: it's so blue. a distinct shade.

caridad: the blue of a vein. that's a color branded into the very flesh of your eyes. you were remembering ...

maria: i wasn't remembering anything.

caridad: *(singing.) es imposible borrar*
los recuerdos del mar
no se puede olividar
los recuerdos del mar.
imposible dejar
imposible escapar
imposible olvidar ...

do you remember now?

maria: i remember the caribbean. turbulent. like a hurricane was happening.

caridad: and the story? do you remember that? a small fishing boat is rocking on the surface. three men: juan a, juan b, and juan c sitting there.

maria: the story of *la caridad.*

caridad: they are looking for her. the drowning girl. they scan the surface. the green and blue that turns grey and white in the middle of a storm. they search for anything. a hand, an arm, her dark black hair fanning out among the waves. we hear them talking. we hear them asking: what caused her to do this? what caused her to go out into the sea on a night like this?

maria: wait. that's not the story.

caridad: it's my story. it is also your story.

(she extends a hand holding a razor.)

caridad: take it.

(maria reaches out her hand.)

caridad: you long for it. you desire it. you crave it. i can tell.

(maria retreats her hand.)

maria: no. i don't think so.

caridad: i am your mother. that was my arm in the picture. you were remembering me. you were always remembering me.

maria: you are not, nor will you ever be my mother.

caridad: es imposible escapar, marea.

(she folds up the razor. darkness.)

13.

(in the darkness, we hear regla's voice.)

regla: *en tu silencio,* (in your silence)
escuchame. (hear me.)
en tu oscuridad, (in your darkness)
mirame. (see me.)
obedézcame (obey me)
con tu alma, (with your soul)
con tu mente (with your mind)
y con tu corazón. (and with your heart.)
no es a un hombre (it isn't a man)
que se debe obedecer, (you must obey)
si no a dios el señor. (but god, our lord.)
maria ... (maria ...)
maria ... (maria ...)
despierta ... (wake up ...)

claudia: she's waking.

14.

(the lights come up on maria in her bed. next to her are regla and claudia.)

maria: *abuela?*

regla: maria.

claudia: i called her.

maria: what?

regla: you have been sick.

maria: when did you learn english?

claudia: she's always spoken english to me on the phone. *(to regla.)* she's terrible. she told me you don't speak any english at all.

regla: i do what i can.

maria: we always spoke spanish. we never spoke english.

claudia: she refuses to speak *español* around me. we do a little *italiano*.

regla: are you italian?

claudia: me? god, no. iowa.

regla: i am sure it's very pretty. iowa.

claudia: you don't have to say that.

maria: what are you doing here? *¿que haces?*

regla: *(to claudia.)* my granddaughter always liked the italian. i do not have any idea *porqué*.

claudia: they're similar, though, aren't they?

regla: that is what they say.

maria: they're completely different.

regla: spanish is so beautiful, so useful, so important if you want good work. that is what i hear. i do not hear any person saying that they must learn the italian. but what do i know? i am a miserable old woman. i am old fashioned and not used to the modern ways. she is the one who knows it all. i suppose she is the expert.

maria: you suppose?

claudia: *cara*, don't get all crazy. you've had a rough couple of nights. *(to regla.)* she was clutching her inhaler in her sleep. it must be the smoking.

regla: she smokes?

maria: claudia, i can't believe you would do this.

claudia: you were out cold for two days. what the hell do you expect me to do?

regla: relax yourself, maria, and i will make you *manzanilla*. that always calmed you.

claudia: *manzanilla*?

maria: *(to claudia.)* chamomile. *(to regla.)* *no quiero.*

regla: *(hissing.)* *no seas majadera conmigo, hija.*

maria: claudia, where's my inhaler?

regla: *(to claudia.)* she doesn't need the medicine. she needs to calm herself. she is too nervous.

maria: didn't i tell you she's a witch? get me the inhaler. *(to regla.)* *estas en mi casa.*

regla: *cuidate, que estas muy equivocada.*

(claudia hands maria the inhaler and she takes a hit.)

maria: my grandfather died because of her. he got sick. instead of a doctor, she brought him a priest.

regla: *(to claudia.)* please, can you boil some water for the tea?

claudia: i don't think we have any chamomile.

(regla pulls out a bag from her purse.)

regla: i brought it with me. it is a special blend.

maria: *(getting out of bed.)* claudia, don't.

(regla presses her back down on the bed.)

regla: *quedate! (to claudia.)* the water, please.

claudia: *si, señora. (to maria.)* you're being impossible.

(claudia leaves the room. regla walks over to the door and closes it.)

maria: when did you learn to speak english?

regla: since you left me, i practiced every day. i was waiting. i was always waiting. day after day. hour after hour. i was very patient. i knew it was impossible for you to escape from me. i knew you would come back to me. i was like a mother to you. salute me the way i deserve, *hija.* press your lips to my cheek.

maria: you have not changed a bit.

regla: i am still your grandmother. i don't care who you think you are, but i still deserve respect.

maria: i will ask you very politely then. *abuela*, please go. i do not want to see you.

regla: but i cannot leave you like this. sick. in bed. i am taking you home.

maria: this is my home

regla: your home is with me. in miami.

maria: no!

regla: how dare you say no to me?

maria: i don't want to go back to that horrible place. that backwards place. i never belonged there.

regla: of course you did. you are my family.

maria: i wanted nothing more than to escape. to get the hell out and not come back to the … the ridiculousness. it's like … a beast. it's a pair of claws wrapped around your neck, choking you.

regla: and what about here? you are not happy in this house.

maria: i am extremely happy.

regla: you aren't married.

maria: i don't intend to be.

regla: a woman should not be alone. we need to take care of things. things that belong to us. i don't know what i would have done if i did not have you with me after i lost your grandfather and your mother.

maria: i take care of claudia.

regla: that kind of caring is not enough.

maria: why don't you tell me what you mean.

regla: *no es mi lugar–*

maria: *–no. no es tu lugar–*

regla: –there are cuts on your legs ... and *la americana* told me she's asked you to move out.

(silence.)

regla: you have tried to run away. you have tried to escape. but you haven't gone anywhere at all. i am going to go into the kitchen and see if your ... *amiguita* needs help with the *manzanilla*.

maria: you do that.

(regla exits. regla enters the kitchen and looks at claudia, who is arranging the tea cups.)

regla: i will make the tea.

claudia: it's no bother.

regla: i will make the tea.

claudia: okay.

(she exits the kitchen and goes back into the bedroom. regla begins to make the tea.)

claudia: she kicked me out of the kitchen.

maria: what part of "i never want to see her again" didn't you understand?

claudia: you were unconscious. i had to do something. i thought she could take care of you. i'm sorry.

maria: she wants me to go back to miami.

claudia: you're a grown woman. she can't control you. she can't make you do anything you don't want. but it's really not a bad idea. get away for a while. spend some time with her. you're her only family.

maria: you actually want me to go with her?

claudia: look, i think instead of you moving out, we just spend some time apart. leave your things here and come back. just think about it.

maria: she wasn't supposed to come here! she doesn't exist here! miami doesn't exist here!

claudia: *cara* …

maria: i'm being sucked back! don't you see that?

(regla appears in the door, holding the tea.)

regla: maria, drink this.

maria: claudia, please, help me …

claudia: you're acting like a child, *cara.*

regla: *(to claudia.)* please hold her down.

(claudia holds down maria as regla advances with the tea. there is a struggle. regla expertly pries maria's mouth open and pours the tea down her throat.)

maria: it's burning me … i'm being sucked back.

regla: sleep. you will feel better when you wake up. and then we can go home.

maria: *(crying.)* claudia … help …

claudia: *(to regla.)* what was in that tea?

(the tea begins to take effect. maria struggles out of bed. regla tries to grab her.)

regla: *maria, calmate.*

(maria musters whatever strength she has left and pushes regla away.)

maria: see here. both of you. i will not go. i will not.

(she runs out of the bedroom and into the bathroom, locking the door behind her.)

regla: give her time.

(darkness.)

15.

(the living room. regla is packing maria's suitcase. claudia stands nearby. she has been crying.)

claudia: i am worried. she's been in there too long.

regla: she will come out.

claudia: this has been a huge mistake. i shouldn't have called you.

regla: and why not?

claudia: *señora*, please. i mean this with respect. i've never seen her this upset. i don't think she should go anywhere. at least not like this.

regla: and since when do you know what's best?

claudia: she is my ... *friend.* is that what we're calling it?

regla: i am not blind.

claudia: then, please, do not question my judgment.

regla: your judgment does not have any meaning next to that of god's.

claudia: whatever you say.

(she lights a cigarette.)

regla: i would prefer it if you didn't smoke.

claudia: of course, you are a guest.

regla: you are the guest. i am family.

claudia: whatever.

(she continues to smoke.)

regla: i don't now what you think this thing is. she is mine. she is tied to me.

claudia: then tell me this: what is her favorite movie?

regla: i don't see what that has to do with anything.

(claudia produces the dvd for l'avventura.)

claudia: *l'avventura.* directed by michelangelo antonioni. released in 1960. starring monica vitti. antonioni called it *"un giallo in rovescia,"* a noir in reverse. where the victim is never found and the crime is never solved. this is the movie she loves most of all. i always thought if i understood this movie, i'd understand her. but it's almost impossible to understand, *señora.*

regla: you don't understand her because you do not love her.

claudia: that's not true.

regla: you were kicking her out.

claudia: ok. but tell me. do you think she loves you?

regla: i love her. much more than someone like you can. she is my granddaughter. she is not a movie.

claudia: what do you do when she suddenly wakes up one day and something has changed? she says she hears voices. she cuts herself up with a razor.

regla: this does not concern you.

claudia: when she was out cold, she was calling out for a "caridad."

regla: this is none of your business!

claudia: who is caridad?

(silence.)

regla: it is *la caridad del cobre.* she is the patron saint of cuba. there is a story that three fishermen, three men named juan were out in the ocean and they thought they saw a drowning girl, but it was the statue of the virgin floating in the waves. it was a miracle, the holy mother appearing to them like that. there is a shrine to her in cobre where people ask her for miracles.

claudia: does that work?

regla: no. no it doesn't. there are no miracles. only curses.

claudia: what happened to maria's mother?

regla: *(running to the door.) ¡maria! ¡abre esta puerta ahora!*

claudia: why won't you tell maria?

regla: and who do you think you are making those demands on me? i will not answer you. i have nothing to say to you.

claudia: what happened?

regla: *¡te dije que no! ¡asquerosa! ¡desgraciada!*

(she starts sobbing, clutching her stomach as pain wells up in her.)

regla: you have no right. no one has any right. *(she winces, and then steadies herself.) sagrado sea el dolor, amado sea el dolor, sanctificado sea el dolor, glorificado sea el dolor.*

(she is composed again. she faces the bathroom door.)

regla: maria!

claudia: she was right about you. absolutely.

regla: tell her to open this door.

claudia: you do it. i'm watching a movie.

(she pops in the dvd for l'avventura.)

regla: *¡maria, abre la puerta!*

16.

(maria is slumped against the bathroom door, drugged from the tea. time is slowly suspended. imagery from l'avventura flickers throughout.)

maria: think of what you believe in. *l'avventura.* antonioni. lea masari plays anna. gabriele ferzetti plays her boyfriend sandro. and monica vitti plays her best friend, claudia. claudia … they are on an island. an old, ruined island made almost entirely of rock. anna tells sandro, "i've grown used to being alone." her hair wild. wind whipping her. waves crashing against her. "i need to spend some time alone," she repeats. but sandro does not listen. sandro does not understand. and then … the weather changes. anna has disappeared. claudia looks for anna. "anna!" she calls. the island filled with her voice. "anna! anna!" but anna is not trapped in a ravine nor is her body floating dead in the ocean. she has escaped the island. she has achieved a clean and perfect escape.

(freeze frame on monica vitti's face in closeup. the woman appears.)

woman: and do you believe that is possible? to escape an island without paying the price?

maria: what price?

caridad: drowning.

maria: all successful people are escape artists. that is what i believe in.

(over the following, monica vitti's image slowly turns into a closeup of barbara steele in la maschera del demonio.)

caridad: in that house. in miami. there was a door that was never meant to be opened. you were told: do not! *¡ni te atrevas!* you were terrified, reaching out for the doorknob in the dark. and the knob would grow slicker, slippery with your sweat. you wondered what was behind the door. another set of rooms with people living there? that other set of rooms, that place, that city, that country that lay behind the door you called it cuba. you draw pictures of cuba as you imagine it. people roaming the streets, just this side of dead, blood pouring out slowly from two tiny puncture wounds at their necks. every day you imagined one person: lourdes or josefina or consuelo or whoever. a nurse or a schoolteacher or a maid walking down the street, holding her purse, looking for her lipstick. she wonders what she'd like for dinner or what she'd watch on television. and then, a frigid shadow falls over her. close up on her face looking up, terrified. close up on his eyes, like two tiny lit coals. close up on his mouth stretched back to reveal long, thick incisors and a tiny stream of saliva sliding out. she runs. she runs as fast as she can until she gets to the ocean. and she wonders. does she leap in and drown or does she stay on the island with the vampire? but before she decides, the vampire sinks his teeth into lourdes or josephina or consuelo or whoever.

this was cuba. do you remember?

(silence.)

maria: hand on the doorknob ... i wanted to make it turn. and one day it happended. i opened my mouth. because i felt. i knew ... *"mamá?"* and then ... whispering. the door began to speak.

caridad: marea ...

maria: someone calling. it was like my name. i thought they were saying maria and i just hadn't heard right.

caridad: marea ...

maria: i was tearing my hair. clawing my skin, wanting to make it bleed. i craved blood. i forced myself to stop. i should not be doing this. i was *una* *traviesa. una pecadora.* i left the door. left cuba locked away. i made myself forget.

(there is a knocking sound. the image of barbara steele begins to fade.)

regla: *(offstage.) ¡maria, abre la puerta!*

caridad: come closer.

maria: i'm afraid.

caridad: there's no need to be.

maria: you're going to hurt me.

(caridad pulls out the razor.)

caridad: *tesoro mio.* you know i could never hurt you. give in. stop resisting.

(silence as maria reaches for the razor. when she grabs the razor she slashes at caridad.)

maria: stay away!

(blood appears over caridad's belly.)

caridad: *¿que hiciste, marea?*

maria: what you wanted to do to me.

(she grabs the doorknob of the bathroom door.)

caridad: don't leave me again.

maria: i'm escaping.

caridad: it's impossible, *hija.* there is no escape.

maria: there is always an escape.

(maria reaches for a door, she opens it and …)

part two
(there should be no intermission between parts one and two)

1.

(... steps out of the bathroom into her home in miami. she listens. there is no one. she stands in the living room where there is a door to a bathroom and a door to a bedroom, but maria moves to a third door. her relationship to the door is one part incredible fear and one part insatiable desire. she runs her hands over the door. silence. she tries the doorknob.)

maria: make it turn ... make it turn.

(the door does not open. she puts her ear to the door. silence. she steps away. regla emerges from the kitchen.)

regla: what are you doing?

maria: *(letting go of the doorknob.)* nothing.

2.

regla: you were in the bathroom for an hour.

maria: i lost track of time.

regla: you are lost somewhere inside your head. always. *(she feels maria's skin).* you are warm. did you shower with hot water?

maria: only cold. like our spiritual director says.

regla: did you use the brush?

maria: until i bled.

regla: very good. let me see your nails.

(maria extends her hand.)

maria: i filed them perfectly.

(regla hands maria a dress.)

regla: i finally finished the stitching. i want you to wear this tonight. it is the feast day of la caridad.

maria: thank you, *abuela.*

regla: try it on. i want to see how it fits.

(maria removes her robe. regla holds the dress out for her and she steps into it. the fit is unflattering.)

maria: please help me with the back.

regla: of course. *(she zips maria up and feels the fabric with her hand.)* this is very good fabric. very strong.

maria: it scratches.

regla: that is good. the discomfort will serve as a meditation. the dress fits well. you can wear it with your good shoes. *(she sets the shoes out for maria.)* i need to get back to dinner. excuse me.

(blackout.)

3.

(the darkness is broken by candlelight illuminating a statue of la caridad del cobre. *regla and maria sit on either side, reading the lives of the saints. maria, however, has an italian phrase book hidden inside her copy.)*

regla: *(reading.) santa lucia* could not marry the young nobleman as she had offered her virginity to god. she hoped he would understand. she hoped he would see. she did not want to be a wife. she dreamed of being a martyr.

maria: *learn to speak italian.*

(music. giovanni fusco's score to l'avventura. monica appears. she is very chic. black and white imagery from l'avventura flickers throughout.)

monica: first lesson. translate. "listen to me."

maria: *sentame.*

regla: the nobleman did not accept lucia's refusal. he asked again and she refused again. each refusal angered him more and more until he began making threats.

monica: "understand me."

maria: *capiscame.*

regla: lucia realized she could manipulate this filthy pagan into being the instrument of her glory. the nobleman would deliver her martyrdom. and this would bring her the greatest pleasure.

monica: "find me."

maria: *troviame.*

regla: the nobleman accused lucia as a christian. she was sentenced to a brothel to be defiled, debased, deflowered. but such would not be a glorious enough martyrdom, so god made lucia immobile and no guard could take her to the brothel.

monica: "touch me."

maria: *tocchiame.*

regla: her eyes were carved out of her head with the dullest of blades, but this too was an unacceptable martyrdom for such a saint as lucia, so god restored her eyesight.

monica: "look at me."

maria: *vediame.*

regla: lucia was subjected to hundreds of tortures. her flesh burned, sliced, and bitten. in the end, she was sentenced to be tortured and raped for thirty-three days straight and lucia knew this would bring her the greatest pleasure, the most incendiary delight.

monica: "embrace me."

maria: *abbracciame.*

regla: every jolt of pain

monica: "kiss me."

maria: *baciame.*

regla: every second of squalor

monica: "open me."

maria: *aprisame.*

regla: sweeter than the last

monica: "taste me."

maria: *gustame.*

regla: until the end of the thirty-third day when her god, her most beautiful god would collect her in his strong and able arms.

monica: "worship me."

maria: no … save me.

monica: are you sure?

regla: maria?

monica: ciao, bella.

(she disappears.)

regla: maria?

maria: si, *abuela.*

regla: are you listening to me?

maria: yes. of course. *(she flips the pages of the book.)* santa clara.

regla: i was not reading *santa clara.*

(she walks over to maria and notices the italian phrase book.)

regla: what is this? *(she opens the book.)* italian?

maria: give that back!

regla: what are you doing with this? what for do you need to speak the italian?

maria: someone gave me that book. it was a gift.

regla: who gave this to you? tell me.

maria: *abuela*, please give it back to me. it's very very–

regla: –maria, you know there are no secrets in this house–

maria: –diame il mio libro!

regla: i don't want to hear you speaking the italian! *¡jamás!*

maria: why not?

regla: *(pocketing the book.)* just go to your room.

maria: you have no right to take that book! it's mine!

regla: *¿quién es la que manda en esta casa?* you are being foolish! stupid! wasting your time! what is the point of speaking the italian? it is like your mother and ... *(stopping herself.)*

maria: she spoke italian?

regla: she did a lot of things she shouldn't have done.

maria: *abuela,* tell me. what was she like?

regla: she was misguided ...

maria: tell me.

regla: there's nothing to tell.

maria: you blame me.

regla: don't say that. you are my granddaughter.

maria: i am a bastard.

regla: i don't want to hear that ugly word. you are my flesh. my blood. you're not ... not ...

maria: then who was my father?

(regla grabs the statue of la caridad and begins blowing out the candles.)

maria: if i'm not a bastard, was my father?

regla: *(barking.)* *¡maria, por favor, callate!*

(she realizes in her anger she's let the statue slip, smashing to the ground.)

regla: *¡mi estatua!*

(she gathers the pieces.)

maria: *abuela,* i'm sorry.

regla: *fue tu culpa, maria.* all of it is your fault.

(maria storms into her room. blackout.)

4.

(maria in her room. she composes a letter.)

maria: dear monica. it must seem strange hearing from me since it's been a long time since high school and those afternoons we had. i found an article about your movie in an old newspaper in the office of our church. it was a miracle considering i have been thinking about ways to find you for so long ... *cara*, i must talk to you. don't write. don't call. come here. there is no other way since she watches me all the time. find me, monica. come back to me ... i need your help. i'm afraid this letter would do as much good as the ones castaways put in bottles, but i hope ...

regla's voice: maria, i brought you *manzanilla.*

(regla opens the door to maria's room, maria quickly hides the letter.)

regla: i made it how you like it with a little bit of honey.

(she extends the cup, maria takes it.)

regla: you must forgive me. i don't like to trouble you with stories from the past. your heart doesn't need my pains.

maria: i'm sorry, *abuela.* i know how hard it must be. but i wish you would tell me more about–

regla: shhhh ... you don't need to take care of me. *(she kisses maria.)*

maria: your statue?

regla: we'll get some glue. drink your *manzanilla* and get some sleep.

(maria drinks the tea. regla leaves, closing the door behind her. maria and regla are both silent, listening for the other. they wait for a bit, then regla silently opens the unopenable door.)

maria: *(rapidly chanting.) capiscame, troviame, tocchiame, vediame, abbracciame, baciame, aprisame ...*

(giovanni fusco's score for l'avventura *plays. monica appears. black and white imagery from* l'avventura *flickers throughout.)*

monica: have you been using the phrasebook i gave you?

maria: i've kept it with me all the time.

monica: you should practice more.

maria: i'm nervous.

monica: don't be afraid.

maria: my grandmother ...

monica: don't think about her. listen to the music. pretend we're in rome and kiss me.

maria: i wish we were really there. we could run away. we could escape.

monica: what for? wherever i am, that is rome.

(monica disappears. the manzanilla begins to take effect maria lays down on the bed.)

maria: *(singing.) es imposible dejar*
los recuerdos del mar ...
imposible escapar ...
imposible escapar ...
imposible escapar ...

(caridad's voice is heard.)

caridad: marea …

maria: *¿mamá?*

caridad: *abre la puerta* …

maria: *abre … la … puerta* …

(she passes out.)

5.

(in the darkness we hear regla's voice.)

regla: *quedate en tu oscuridad.* (stay in your darkness.)
quedate en tu silencio. (stay in your silence.)
quedate en tu miseria. (stay in your misery.)
sagrado sea el dolor. (the pain is sacred.)
amado sea el dolor. (the pain is loved.)
sanctificado sea el dolor. (the pain is blessed.)
glorioso sea el dolor. (the pain is glorious.)
duermete, maria. (go to sleep, maria.)
duermete. (go to sleep.)

6.

(the darkness is broken by candlelight illuminating a mended statue of la
caridad del cobre. *regla and maria sit on either side, reading the lives of the
saints. caridad is distracted. she looks at the statue.)*

maria: i tried to fix it.

regla: it's not the same.

maria: i'm sorry.

regla: *no te preocupes.* just read.

maria: *¿santa barbara?*

regla: *(shrugging her shoulders.) me da lo mismo.*

maria: *(reading.) santa barbara* could feel the blade. she could sense the shiver of the sword as her father held it to her neck. pulse against steel. the moment, the waiting, the second he hesitated wondering if he could do this to his own daughter.

(regla caresses the statue. caridad appears.)

maria: she who was so wicked to defy him.

caridad: *es imposible dejar*
los recuerdos del mar.
es imposible escapar
los recuerdos del mar.

maria: all in the name of this man.

regla: *hija?*

maria: this imaginary god. this jesus christ.

caridad: *mamá.*

(caridad sits at her mother's feet and places her head in her lap.)

maria: and in that second, barbara thought of the water in the bath house her father had built. she thought of herself naked, standing waist deep in the water. her skin gathered in gooseflesh as she watched the light penetrate the three windows of the bathhouse. the trinity. three beams of sunlight caressing her shoulders, her breasts. she had no need for the touch of any living creature. she had transcended beyond such ordinary and petty things. she was ether. she was evaporating there in the water, slowly disappearing every day.

caridad: *tengo miedo, mamá. creo que algo terrible me ha pasado.*
(mother, i am afraid. i think something terrible has happened to me.)

regla: *(stroking caridad's hair.) nada te pasara. el señor te proteje.* (nothing will happen to you. the lord will protect you.)

maria: so she did not feel the blade. she did not notice when her father drew his arm up, bringing the blade down hard on her neck. first cut. he raised his arm again, bringing it down even harder.

caridad: *tengo miedo, mamá. nadie me ha protejido.* (mother, i am afraid. no one has protected me.)

maria: second cut.

caridad: *nadie.* (no one.)

regla: (writhing in pain.) *preciosa* (precious.)
querida (beloved.)
purisima (purest.)
mi unico tesoro (my only treasure.)
mi unico amor. (my only love.)
mi linda. (my lovely.)
mi hija. (my daughter)

caridad: *nadie.* (no one).

maria: blood from the jugular stained the blade, sprayed his tunic.

regla: *¡ay!*

maria: arm raised again, bringing it down rapidly for the third and final cut.

caridad: *es tu culpa, madre.* (it's your fault, mother.)

maria: three blows to sever the bone, the muscle, the sinew.

regla: *¡mi hija, no me dejes!* (my child, don't leave me!)

(caridad disappears.)

maria: three blows for the father, the son and the holy ghost.

(the unopenable door begins to rattle. the doorknob begins to shake.)

maria: *abuela*, what's happening?

regla: nothing. nothing is happening. you should go to your room.

maria: the door. someone is behind it.

regla: get those ideas out of your head. they are fantasies!

(the door rattling intensifies with the sound of a hand banging on the door.)

maria: it's her, isn't it?

(maria runs to the door. trying to open it.)

maria: it's her! it's her!

regla: *(striking maria.)* maria, no! don't touch that door! ¡ni te atrevas!

(the rattling stops. maria is immobile on the ground. she doesn't say a word. she does not cry.)

regla: i will make you some *manzanilla*. you have to sleep.

maria: i don't want *manzanilla*. i don't want to sleep. i want to know what's behind that door.

regla: absolutely nothing.

maria: then show me.

regla: help me clean up. blow out the candles.

maria: i'm not *una inocente!* i'm thirty years old. you treat me like a stupid child.

regla: stop behaving like one!

maria: i can't live here. i can't live in this house.

regla: this is your home.

maria: not with so many secrets it isn't.

regla: those secrets are mine. this house is mine. what's behind that door is mine. i don't care how old you are. it doesn't mean anything.

(the doorbell rings. they are both frozen.)

regla: who is that?

maria: i don't know.

regla: are you expecting someone?

maria: no, of course not. are you?

(the doorbell rings again. maria looks through the peephole.)

maria: she came!

regla: who is it?

maria: *che bella donna. (to regla.)* i need to change. let her in while i go put something on.

regla: what is going on?

(maria runs into her room while regla, petrified, opens the door, letting monica into the house.)

7.

monica: it's a pleasure, *señora.*

regla: and who are you?

monica: i'm monica. i went to school with maria.

regla: catholic school?

monica: where else?

regla: i don't remember you.

monica: well, i don't remember you either. so that makes us even.

regla: do you still live in miami?

monica: new york. i produce films.

regla: i don't like films.

monica: me neither.

regla: then why do you do it?

monica: i won an award. once. years ago. maybe i'll win another one. where's maria?

regla: in her room. i will tell her you're here.

monica: not yet. i need to freshen up. *(she grabs the doorknob to the forbidden door.)* is this the *toletta?*

regla: no. that door doesn't open.

(regla points to the bathroom door.)

regla: that is the one that you want.

monica: did you say this door doesn't open.

regla: that is what i said.

monica: how odd. *scuzi.*

(she enters the bathroom. maria comes out of her room. she is as well-dressed as a she could possibly be.)

maria: do i look all right?

regla: i don't like her.

maria: i changed my dress three times.

regla: she is not the sort of person who should be seen visiting us. people could talk.

maria: she's just my friend monica from school.

regla: you didn't have any friends.

maria: she gave me the book you stole. my italian phrasebook.

(monica steps out of the bathroom in a cloud of cigarette smoke. she is wearing shades and looking even more chic.)

monica: *ciao, bella!*

maria: monica …

monica: *dove è il mio baccio?*

(they kiss, continental style.)

monica: *bellisima!*

maria: you don't mean that.

monica: of course i do. walk around and let me take a look at you.

(maria walks around. regla stands back, dumbfounded.)

monica: you still have your legs, *cara.* and an eye for shoes …

maria: these are cheap. pieces of trash. look at yours!

monica: my friend manolo …

regla: and who is this manolo? another friend from school?

(monica stares at regla with sincere curiosity.)

monica: maria, your grandmother is so ... *simpatica*. now! i'm positively dying for a chianti.

(she pulls out a bottle of wine from her bag.)

monica: you are going to love this. it's absolutely voluptuous.

regla: you put that away. there is no drinking in this house.

maria: it's just some wine, *abuela*. i haven't seen monica since i was in high school.

regla: i don't want to see my granddaughter behaving *como una qualquiera. señorita*, i am sorry i am going to have to be rude ... *(she opens the front door.)* ... but you are not welcome here ... and maria and i are late for our appointment with our spiritual director.

monica: *(pointing to maria's room.)* is this your room?

maria: yes.

(monica steps into maria's bedroom.)

monica: get in here, then. the old woman is starting to freak me out.

regla: *(rushing to maria's room.)* i beg your pardon!

monica: *(blocking regla's path.)* private party, *señora*, and you're not on the list.

maria: *abuela, no te procupes.*

monica: *addio.*

(she closes the door, locking it.)

regla: *(pounding the door.)* maria! maria!

(she puts her ear to the door and listens in.)

8.

(maria's room.)

monica: look at me.

maria: i'm afraid to.

monica: why afraid?

maria: i'm shaking.

monica: your lip is trembling … just like it used to.

(they are still, then maria runs over to monica and embraces her, tightly. monica is taken aback and then returns the embrace. a moment. silence.)

regla: *(knocking on the door.)* ¿maria, por que le pusiste el pestillo a la puerta? ¿que haces?*

(maria releases herself from the embrace.)

maria: *abuela, por favor …*

monica: let's put on some music.

regla: maria!

monica: i don't want her listening in.

(she reaches into her purse and pulls out a cd.)

monica: nino rota.

(monica puts the cd in maria's stereo.)

monica: "are you dancing, maria? you're in luck! i am the best dancer in rome!"

(monica dances a bit of a mambo. on the other side of the door, regla opens the forbidden door with a key from her pocket. she opens the door and steps inside, closing it behind her.)

maria: i remember looking at film stills listening to this music with you, trying to guess how monica vitti sounded. how she moved. we had to make the pictures move in our heads. remember?

monica: have you changed at all, maria?

maria: i still haven't seen l'avventura.

(monica produces a wrapped package from her purse. it is a dvd.)

monica: i was afraid of that.

maria: we don't have a television.

monica: i was afraid of that too.

maria: was the movie like we imagined?

monica: no movie was like how we imagined. not a single one. but i still love the music.

maria: it's like being in your car again. do you think about that?

monica: sometimes.

maria: no. always.

monica: it was a very clean arrangement. secret. you and me somewhere near the ocean. in some parking lot. kissing. smoking. listening to music. kissing some more. over and over. simple.

maria: i replay those afternoons with you in my head. it's on an infinite loop.

monica: what a movie!

maria: my memories had to become my movies.

monica: i received your letter.

maria: i'm so glad.

monica: what's the matter?

maria: i wanted to see you again. i wanted ...

(she is unsure. silence.)

maria: i wanted to look at you.

monica: oh, god. i have to confess this whole getup is something i hardly do anymore. i ... um ... laid it on pretty thick out there for the old woman.

maria: i think about your life. i try to imagine if i lived it. if i left here. if i went to new york and did something with myself ...

monica: something? like what?

maria: i don't know. anything. go to the movies for one. tell me about new york. tell me what it's like

monica: i really don't want to ruin your fantasy.

maria: that would be impossible.

monica: oh, it's very possible. for one, i hardly go to the movies. i hate going to the movies. *(she laughs to herself.)* when i went to new york, i was hellbent on creating these perfect little films with perfect little women wearing perfect little black dresses and shades and falling in love with men wearing these perfect little black suits. i wanted films that were sharp and stylish and black and white. clean. i had a hard on for the *via veneto*, you know? of course you know. i wore those black dresses. i smoked a lot. i had wild affairs. i learned what to drink. very well. i wanted to be cool and have everything be *cosi interessante*. but i was young and by young, i mean stupid.

maria: i don't think that's stupid.

monica: *cara* ...

maria: it's not stupid to want things.

monica: of course not, but we have to live with certain realities. wanting life to be a black and white movie is sort of crazy. it's not 1960 anymore ... as much as i'd love that. i'd be able to smoke in a bar for one. but those girls ... monica vitti and all that ... they don't exist. that girl i wanted to be. she doesn't exist.

maria: why did you come here?

monica: your letter. you asked me to come. and i had to come.

maria: i wanted you to come back. i wanted it to be like it used to be

monica: we're not in high school any more.

maria: no. we're not.

(she's quiet.)

maria: i was hoping you'd help me get out of here.

monica: help you?

maria: take me back with you. loan me the money to go to new york. let me stay with you. i will pay you back. i'll do anything ...

monica: oh. i ... uh ... oh, god, *cara.*

maria: you need to help me.

monica: i want to. i want to take care of you, but we haven't seen each other, we haven't spoken in years!

maria: but it's me! i'm the same person!

monica: i'm not! i'm just … i don't know. i don't know. you know, when i got your letter, i cried for hours.

maria: cried? why?

monica: you still thought i was … i was this person i used to be. you still thought i was young.

maria: but you are.

monica: i've been living with all this disappointment. these expectations. i can't bring you with me–

maria: –no, please–

monica: –i couldn't disappoint you too.

maria: how can you sit there and tell me you would disappoint me? look at this house. do you think i'm happy here? do you think i'm going to get to new york and wish i never left this place?

monica: i should go. this was a bad idea.

maria: no. please.

monica: this music. this wine. i was hoping if i saw you again, if you saw me like you did, i could walk out of here and go home and i could … well, i could stop crying when i read letters. i could like making films again.

maria: *sentame.*

monica: you should leave here yourself. go somewhere else if you're unhappy.

maria: *vediame.*

monica: you don't need me. you don't need these movies. these fantasies …

maria: *capiscame.*

monica: *troviame.*

(silence.)

maria: you're the only person i've ever loved.

monica: i always thought you looked a bit like lea masari in *l'avventura.* staring at the ocean. a little lost. a little scared. i always felt so different from you. so foreign. so i ran away from you.

maria: why?

monica: i was afraid i'd drown. *(she grabs a cigarette.)* want one?

maria: she'd smell it.

monica: all the more reason. you're a grown woman, maria. you do what you want.

(maria takes the cigarette.)

monica: *brava!*

maria: *bravissima!*

(they smoke.)

monica: i'm sorry i disappointed you.

maria: you didn't disappoint me.

(monica kisses maria. regla comes out of the forbidden door, closing it behind her. the door makes a sound. all three women freeze. monica turns down the music. a beat. regla moves to maria's door to listen in.)

monica: *(whispered.)* what was that?

maria: *(whispered.)* the door next to the bathroom.

monica: the old woman says it doesn't open.

maria: it does. she has the key.

monica: what do you think's behind there?

maria: i have no idea. i've never been allowed to even touch the doorknob.

(pause.)

maria: can i tell you something? sometimes i hear things behind the door.

monica: like what?

maria: at first, i thought i was imagining it. i was a child when i first heard it. *"marea, abre la puerta."*

monica: you mean maria?

maria: no, they said, "marea." the tide …

monica: who do you think is calling you?

(silence.)

maria: my mother.

monica: you think your mother is behind that door?

maria: no. of course not. i mean … that would be impossible, wouldn't it? that would be … it's just my imagination. she left me when i was a baby. of course, i would think …

monica: but she's keeping something behind that door. aren't you ever curious?

maria: she would kill me.

(she looks at her cigarette.)

maria: i want to find out. i want to open that door. tonight.

monica: how?

maria: you could help me pick the lock. you look like the kind of girl who could do that sort of thing with a bobby pin or something.

monica: well, of course, but that's besides the point. i am not going to pick that lock. you need to stand up to that evil old woman and demand that she give you the keys to that door.

maria: she never will. if i am ever going to get in there, i am going to have to break the door down myself. let's do it! let's do something secret and dangerous. just for old time's sake.

monica: that wasn't what i had in mind.

maria: let's wait until she goes to bed. and then we pick the lock. in the meantime …

monica: let's finish that chianti.

(maria grabs the bottle of chianti and drinks some. monica turns up the music. it's a mambo.)

monica: dance with me.

(they dance close. maria begins to kiss monica's neck. the action is vampiric. monica swoons. lights fade out. in the darkness, we hear a woman breathing. it is caridad. her voice reverberates throughout the darkness.)

caridad: *marea, abre la puerta.*

9.

(when the lights come back up, maria and monica are at the door. it is very late at night. monica has her purse next to her. she pulls out expert lockpicking devices.)

monica: i can't believe i am doing this.

maria: don't be afraid.

monica: your grandmother.

maria: don't think about her. pretend we're in rome. kiss me.

monica: i wish i was really there.

maria: wherever i am, that is rome.

(maria grabs monica and kisses her. the lock gives.)

maria: *bellisimo!*

(the door opens on its own. the sound of running water. they stand there afraid.)

caridad's voice: marea …

monica: what is that?

maria: it's her …

(maria stands frozen.)

monica: c'mon. go inside.

maria: *es imposible escapar …* *(she takes a deep breath.)* ok.

(she decides to step through the door. as she does so, regla's shadow falls over monica. monica gasps. darkness.)

10.

(a small room. black and white photographs on the walls: caridad in cuba. regla in cuba. waves crashing on the malecón, *the sea wall in havana. pictures of a handsome young man. a baby photo of maria, etc. caridad stands in the room, completely disheveled.)*

caridad: fade in …

maria: *¿mamá?*

caridad: you found me.

maria: it's you … but … oh, god, it's you.

(maria walks up to her and touches her. she is hesitant. she puts her arms around caridad. they embrace tightly.)

maria: *(crying.) mamá. mamá. mamá. mamá. mamá.*

caridad: *shhh, hija.* look! look what i have.

(she shows maria a script.)

caridad: shhh … it's a secret.

maria: what is it?

maria: it's a story. a film called *marea.*

maria: a film?

caridad: first scene. marea is visited by a ghost. a ghost that whispers her name. a ghost who keeps her up at night, stealing into her dreams, seizing her body and her mind. second scene. marea becomes insane, possessed. she slices her skin with razors to rid herself of the ghost. but the cuts on her skin, her blood are not enough. third scene: she runs to the ocean, to the waves. she walks into the water until she is pulled under. pulled beneath the sea to stay there forever. he wrote this story for me.

maria: who did?

caridad: he was visiting from italy. i met him on the *malecón*. we were looking at the sea. he said he was making a movie. a story set on an island. i know about islands i told him. and i know all about the ocean. i was told once by a mulatta i would meet a man with blue eyes.

es imposible dejar,
imposible borrar,
imposible escapar
los recuerdos del mar ...

maria: that song. i remember. the caribbean. it was blue. everything was blue.

caridad: his eyes ... they were the color of a vein.

(she claws her arms.)

caridad: *ay! desidero ... desidero ... la sangue ... l'anima.*

maria: *(calming her mother down.)* *mamá, shhh ...*

caridad: i was thirty years old. i was thirty years old.

maria: tell me more about the movie.

caridad: the movie ... he was so beautiful and he had these eyes. i kept looking at them. i was afraid. i thought it was dangerous to look at something too much.

maria: *¿papá?*

caridad: your grandmother hated him. but i was so lonely. so lonely living locked up in that house. she was always looking at me. always grabbing at me. but el italiano. he was ... he was ...

(she starts clawing at herself silently.)

maria: he never made the movie, did he?

caridad: no ... he had to go back to italy. but he promised he'd come back. he's coming back for me and for you and i've been waiting. i've been studying the script. look!

(she pulls back the sleeves of her dress. her arms are lined with lacerations.)

caridad: i know how to drown now like marea does. and now you've come back to me. look at you. *(stroking maria's hair.)* *que linda. mi niña. pequeñita.* i wanted so much ... so much ... marea ... i named you. like the movie.

maria: *mamá* ... why did you go?

caridad: i took you with me to beach. i took you. i didn't want to be alone and i ... i couldn't bring you with me. and i left you. i left you. i left you.

but i didn't know, *hija.* i thought i could destroy my flesh but i didn't know i couldn't destroy my desire for you. the drowning girl must pull others under the surface. but she isn't the villain. no. she is the victim. a victim of a curse! love means drowning. love means suffocating. i tried ... i tried *(she claws her arms.) desidero ... desidero ...*

(maria holds her, trying to steady her.)

maria: *mamá.* it's okay. it's okay.

(caridad claws at maria.)

caridad: i am not that strong. i need you. i crave you. i call out your name every night. i have to claim you as my own.

(maria steps away from her.)

maria: no! look at me. at me. i am not a movie. i am your daughter. don't you love me?

caridad: with all my heart.

(she produces the straight razor.)

maria: then why are you doing this?

caridad: because i understand you, marea. *siete la mia figlia. resa a me ... resa a me ... resa a me.*

(caridad attempts to strike with the razor. regla enters the room.)

regla: maria!

(caridad disappears.)

regla: *¿maria, que haces aqui?*

maria: that is not my name.

regla: i told you to never come here.

maria: my name is marea.

regla: that was a mistake. your name is maria. named after *la virgen. vamonos.*

(maria is still.)

maria: where's monica?

regla: she's gone.

(she tosses monica's sunglasses at maria's feet.)

maria: *¿abuela, que hiciste?*

regla: i sent her away.

maria: monica ...

regla: she had no business in this house and you ... you were never supposed to come into this room!

maria: but my mother ... you never even let me see her pictures.

(regla walks over to maria. maria discovers she's been holding the razor. she also discovers she has cut herself on her arm. regla takes the razor.)

regla: do you see why these pictures are none of your business?

maria: her eyes … her face … *her skin* … they're mine too.

regla: no. you are someone else. i took good care to make sure what happened with your mother would not happen again. i made sure none of her remained in you.

maria: but why? why did it happen?

(regla tends to the cut on maria's arm.)

regla: do you know what it is to long for something so much it makes you crazy? it makes a pain inside of you. it is a woman's right–a divine right–to make sure our memories live on in our children. but i had to beg. i had to plead. i believed in miracles then. but no matter how much i believed, *la virgen* didn't think i deserved what i had desired. i should have known better …

we were cursed, *hija*. i was thirty when i had your mother. she was thirty when she drowned herself. i had no idea what would happen next. i had to protect you.

maria: you were protecting me by making me pray for hours? by taking away anything that could have brought me any pleasure?

regla: you have to sacrifice. you have to suffer to make something of yourself in this world. the little you suffered has not been the same to what i have suffered.

(she raises her skirt to reveal a cilice, a spiked garter used for corporal mortification. around the cilice, her stocking is stained with blood.)

regla: our spiritual director says i can only wear this for two hours a week, but i put this on every day as penance for what i have done. and i wear it so you don't have to. so don't tell me you have suffered. i have taken care of you the way she should have done.

maria: but i have never been happy, *abuela.*

regla: life is pain. it is stupid to think otherwise. you have no idea what it is like. to lose all that is beautiful in your life. to look and see her face everywhere. i could not love your grandfather anymore because he reminded me of her. i did not even want to look at you because you reminded me of her. every time you smiled as a baby it was a dagger in my heart.

maria: i need to go away. i need to start over somewhere else.

regla: and what good would that do? do you think you can escape all this? you will never be happy.

maria: how do you know?

regla: because it is impossible. there is no happiness.

maria: that's what you've forced yourself to believe.

regla: it is the truth. even if you run away, you will never ever leave this house.

maria: then why are you so worried?

regla: who will keep you safe when i am gone?

maria: *(a realization.)* i will.

abuela, i have to leave. my body aches in this house. i cannot breathe.

regla: how can you just leave? just be on your own like that?

maria: i've grown used to being alone. goodbye, *abuela.*

(regla strikes maria. maria strikes her back. regla slowly crumbles. silence.)

regla: you will never be happy. you will never be happy.

(maria grabs the doorknob, time stops.)

11.

maria: hand on doorknob. make it turn. leave the room. leave the house. escape. quickly, completely. as if i was never there. hand on doorknob, i make it turn. but when it opens, i step into a hall. someone is on the other end. i don't know why, but i am compelled. i must chase after her. the hall fills with water. it's harder for me to run and as the water reaches my neck, she turns around and looks at me.

she has my face.

and i realize …

(she opens the door and steps inside.)

maria: i'm home.

(we are back in maria's apartment in new york city. end of part one. regla and claudia are on the other side of the bathroom door. maria is staring into the bathroom mirror. she turns and notices caridad's body on the ground, belly still lacerated.)

maria: *mamá … despierta …*

(caridad opens her eyes. she is weak.)

caridad: *hija.* i thought i was going to lose you again.

maria: i thought i could escape.

caridad: there is only one way to escape.

maria: and what will happen then? will i be happy?

caridad: wouldn't it make you happy to be with me? don't you love me?

maria: but then there would be no story. no marea.

caridad: what story?

maria: havana. exterior. a woman walking down the street, holding her purse, looking for her lipstick. and then, a frigid shadow falls over her. the woman runs. gets to the ocean.

caridad: what happens then?

(there is a knocking sound.)

regla: *¡maria, abre la puerta!*

maria: she dives in.

(she kisses caridad on the mouth.)

caridad: i'm floating …

(caridad disappears.)

regla: *¡maria, abre esta puerta, nos vamos!*

claudia: *cara*, please, open the door!

regla: maria!

maria: that is not my name.

(she takes the razor lying on the floor. she closes it and puts in her pocket. goes back to her reflection into the bathroom mirror.)

maria: this is the face. my true face. my name … *mi nombre es marea.*

(blackout. end of play.)

Contributors

ALEJANDRO MORALES is a playwright based in New York City. **sweaty palms** (1998) was developed at Mabou Mines, where he was a Van Lier Fellow/Artist in residence and received a developmental workshop at South Coast Repertory's Hispanic Playwrights Project (2001), directed by Lisa Portes. **sebastián** (2000) was developed at New Dramatists, INTAR and The Public Theater's New Work Now (2002), directed by Peter DuBois. In addition, **sebastián** was awarded the 2002 New Dramatists Whitfield Cook Award. **the silent concerto** received its first reading at New Dramatists in the fall of 2001, directed by Lisa Portes. A new revision of **the silent concerto** was workshopped by Packawallop Productions at New Dramatists and at Tectonic Theater Project in 2004, directed by Scott Ebersold. The completed version of the play received its world premiere at FringeNYC, 2005. In 2002, he received a commission from the NYSF/Public Theater for a new play, entitled **marea**. It was workshopped at The Public, directed by Annie Dorsen and subsequently at New Dramatists, directed by Debbie Saivetz. He recently adapted Antonio Margheriti's 1964 film **castle of blood,** which received its first public reading at New Dramatists (2006), directed by Scott Ebersold and is being turned into a musical. His current project is **the october project (to laura).** Alejandro received his BFA in Drama from New York Universtity's Tisch School of the Arts. He is co-founder of Packawallop Productions (www.packawallop.org) with Scott Ebersold, a film & theater production company. He is an alumnus of New Dramatists and is a member of the Dramatists Guild. He maintains a blog at lowercaseletter.blogspot.com.

CARIDAD SVICH is author of over forty plays and fifteen translations produced across the US and abroad. Among her key works: *Any Place But Here, Alchemy of Desire/Dead-Man's Blues, Fugitive Pieces, Iphigenia Crash Land Falls...(a rave fable), The Booth Variations, Thrush,* and *The Tropic of X.* She was worked with the Royal Court, Traverse Theatre (Edinburgh), Artheater (Cologne), Mark Taper Forum Theatre, 7 Stages, The Women's Project, Cincinnati Playhouse, Salvage Vanguard Theatre, Seattle Repertory Theatre, among many others. Awards include Radcliffe Institute for Advanced Study "Bunting" Fellowship, TCG/PEW National Theatre Artist Residency, NEA/TCG Playwriting Residency, Rosenthal New Play Prize, National Latino Playwriting Award, Whitfield Cook Prize, and she has been short-listed twice for the PEN USA-West Award in Drama. As a translator, she is chiefly known for her English-language translations of the dramatic works of Federico Garcia Lorca. Her first volume of translations is *Federico Garcia Lorca: Impossible Theater* (Smith & Kraus). She is alumna of New Dramatists, founder of theatre alliance and press NoPassport, contributing editor of *TheatreForum*, and on the editorial team of *Contemporary Theatre Review* (Routledge/UK). Her work as playwright-lyricist, translator and editor is published by TCG, Smith & Kraus, Playscripts Inc., Arte Publico Press, Manchester University Press, Stage & Screen, BackStage Books, Kendall-Hunt, and Alexander Street Press. Her website is www.caridadsvich.com

www.ingramcontent.com/pod-product-compliance
Lightning Source LLC
Chambersburg PA
CBHW031219020726
47499CB00002B/642